The Sequence Dance

Short fiction by
S.B. Borgersen

For information contact:
Unsolicited Press
Portland, Oregon
www.unsolicitedpress.com
orders@unsolicitedpress.com
619-354-8005

Front Cover Design: Kathryn Gerhardt
Editor: S.R. Stewart

ISBN: 978-1-956692-13-6

Sequence: a set of things belonging next to one another on some principle of order

Dancing: performing rhythmic bodily motions to music
Extracted from the Canadian Oxford Dictionary

My mother's definition
Sequence Dancing: a different type of ballroom dancing where couples dance to a named and well-practised sequence of steps to sixteen bars of music. Repeating that sequence five or six times. Moving around the dance floor in the same direction and at the same tempo.

Together.

But really, she adds, you need to see it, to properly understand.

For Jim
and
for Vicki

This mother's love never ceases

The Sequence Dance

1. A to Z

At four o'clock he stopped dithering. Bravado kicked in and he banished his earlier cowardly thoughts. Charles had no doubts at all now. Determined, he packed a bag.

Enough of everything: socks; underwear; shirts; a couple of books and his complete collection of Inspector Morse DVDs—all went into the green plaid holdall. Finally, he pocketed his phone and left the house without writing her a note.

Gemma would arrive home from work at seven and probably wonder where the hell he was, why he wasn't standing at the sink in his blue and white striped apron proudly waving a paring knife over his freshly julienned carrots.

Heaving the holdall into the car, Charles took one last look at the house—the house where he'd lived, pleasantly enough, for 20 years, climbed into the old Morris and slowly pulled away and into the traffic.

It was one of those dense, drizzly days, neither rain nor mist. Just constant dampness. Keeping to the side roads, Charles managed to avoid the early afternoon rush hour and soon found himself on the bypass faced with the decision to take the northbound or the southbound carriageway.

Love. Menacing emasculating love. No one had ever questioned him about the topic and he had never thought to explore it himself either, until recently. Open to suggestions last Thursday he had asked Owen at the pub, "What is love?" he said, quite out of the blue, and Owen had said, "Charley, old boy, I had no idea you cared."

Perhaps it was the way Owen had answered, or the way he looked at Charles. Questions like this didn't very often pop up over a pint. Reaching across the beer-ringed mahogany table, Owen kissed him. Surprising himself, Charles had kissed him back.

Turning into Maple Grove, Charles knew exactly where he was going and why. Until now his life had been safe, routine, humdrum. Voices had sometimes skittered around in his head saying, "Charley old fellow, you've only got one stab at this life, why are you wasting it peeling carrots for the little wifey? Why?"

X marked the spot on the page in the mini A-to-Z Owen slid into Charles's top pocket that night. Yawning, as if to feign a casualness that was not foreign to him, Charles had pushed the map further into his pocket to be more secure, knowing full well he would need it at some point.

Zebra crossings had not figured in the map though, and while Charles did apply the brakes, the roads were slick with drizzle and he had no time to think, let alone swerve to avoid the man who, until a few minutes earlier, had been standing at the kerb anxiously, lovingly, looking out for his arrival.

2. From Coalman's Corner to Eternity

He came to me at three o'clock this morning. Wanting to take me to a party. He is dressed as never before—in leathers. And for a guy of two metres tall, that is one helluva lot of forest green leather.

The party is somewhere I'd never been, with people I'd never met. The music is foreign to me, but a wonky rendition of Bridge Over Troubled Waters tickles a memory somewhere. The booze is all gone. And we'd taken none for the BYOB.

The restaurant across the road is full of all-nighters spilled over from the party. We are turned away. The street vendors are packed up, leaving behind the ever-lingering aroma of charcoal. So we give up until, hey-hey, along Jimmy comes in his van. "Climb in," he says.

The route home is not to home but to some place I've never been. We are dropped at Coalman's Corner.

I'm not sure why I'd worn pale aqua lace tulle, but it is a party dress I guess. Just not anywhere near warm enough for a bleak, Lincolnshire February dawn.

As the sky turns from thistle mauve to orchid pink, I look across towards the Wolds to find the first hints of golds. I turn to him then, to share the wonder.

But he is no longer there.

***

Some say it was madness, others said I was bonkers. But I knew it was the right thing to do. At the time.

Remember when I told you about how the bloody sod left me? At Coalman's Corner? On that freezing February dawn? Well, that wasn't the end of it. More like the start.

You see, his friend Jimmy came back in his van, no longer psychedelic purple. "Climb in," he said. Just like he did that night before the sun rose mauve and pink over the Wolds.

I know, I know, it really was a bonkers thing to do. I knew Jimmy was reckless, impulsive and a tad crazy. But that was what I needed. After all, once you've been dumped at Coalman's Corner, where else is there to go? Right?

We drove all day. Stopping at roadhouses. Stopping to pee behind bushes. Stopping to try our hands at snogging someone new. Then to watch waves crash onto shores—imagining that scene from the black and white movie, *From Here to Eternity*. Foam spraying as high as houses. Playing with rainbows. Not one iota like the flat-ass calm of the dinge-grey Humber.

The Caledonian McBrayne ferry was ready to pull out of Skye as we drove up the ramp. "You still ok with this?" Jimmy said.

I swallowed hard, understanding this was a one-way trip. Madness? Bonkers? No, it was the right thing to do. I've been telling myself that for the past twenty-three years.

3. Mail Order Bride

Norman shaved off his beard and dressed in a shirt and necktie to meet her at the airport. He watched the Arrivals board until her flight number flicked to 'landed'. He breathed deeply, looking around at the other people meeting friends and family. He wished he'd made a card with her name on it so she would know it was him. He wished he'd worn dress shoes instead of his work boots. Norman hoped she was on the flight. He'd heard nothing since he mailed her the ticket.

He clutched the bunch of pink carnations he'd picked up for five dollars at the gas station. He wished now they were the twenty-five-dollar red roses. The doors from the immigration hall slid back and forth as people trickled through. He had her photo in his pocket and every time the doors opened, he took the photo half out of his pocket, glanced at it and then up at the face of each arriving passenger.

She tick-tacked across the marble tiles in four-inch red stilettos and a faux leopard skin coat. Her abundantly ringed fingers with long gold-painted nails pushed a cart overflowing with luggage. Her bright yellow hair was piled on top of her head and held in place with diamanté combs. Norman had never seen anything like it. She didn't look like her photo at all. She certainly didn't look like the sensible woman he thought he'd ordered.

No woman in his life had ever painted their nails. His mother, grandmother and sisters were used to working on the land, helping with the potato crop, helping split wood, or tapping the maple trees for syrup. Whatever the season was, the women were expected to help. Fancy nail polish and high-heeled shoes wouldn't last five minutes.

Norman didn't know what to do. Should he go forward with his bunch of flowers? She was a much larger woman than he expected. In her high-heels she was at least six inches taller than him. Her face told him she would give the orders. He needed a gentle soul mate; someone to cuddle up to at night. Someone to take to the cabin hunting at weekends. Someone to fish for trout with him. Someone to help his mother and sisters.

He imagined what she might say to the outside toilet. To the remoteness of the land, the homestead, to the lack of stores, beauty salons, restaurants. He imagined she would not appreciate his property with the tranquility of the woods, the gentle rippling of the trout stream, or the sweetness of the early morning birdsong. Norman assumed, from the look of her, she was a city girl. Certainly not the bride he had anticipated.

People were thinning out. Most of the passengers had been met. Norman hung back. She looked around, her eyes glinting, resting for a brief moment on each male. She skimmed across Norman as if he did not exist.

Norman stood to leave. He would give the flowers to his mother. The price of the ticket would be his only loss. He would settle for a peaceful life with the family and stop yearning for something more.

And then, as he turned, he saw her, his Helga, sitting quietly, waiting patiently. He didn't know how he'd missed her. But she was there in a navy blue raincoat and brown brogues. She had one small suitcase at her feet.

She smiled up at him, her blue eyes sparkling with excitement and said, "Hello Norman, I am Helga."

And he knew she would love the carnations.

4. Shapes

Jeffrey polishes the spokes on his bike. He has his own yellow duster and a tube of chrome polish that he keeps, along with a small spanner and an inner tube repair kit, in a shoebox under the kitchen sink. He counts the spokes as he works his way around each wheel. He grins a widemouthed grin when he reaches the last dirty spoke without a hiccough and shouts, "Thirty-two."

Interruptions don't sit well with Jeffrey and he doesn't shout quite so gleefully when he has to do a recount. But he always rises to the challenge, flicking his flop of dark hair from his creased brow, pursing his full lips, before counting aloud the cleaned and shining spokes. Then continuing with those yet to be polished and counted. Trying not to let the multitude of triangles in the negative spaces get in the way of his concentration.

This morning's phone call girded him into a flurry. 'Can I speak with Mr. Jeffrey Cross please?'

Jeffrey hesitated, just for a moment, before replying, "It is me, I'm speaking. I'm Jeffrey."

' Mr. Cross, we've received your application and we'd like you to come for interviews and aptitude testing tomorrow morning at 9 am.'

Jeffrey jumped up and down, "Mum, Mum, I will need to wear a shirt and tie," he said. "Do I have one?" He looked down at his grey tee-shirt, his favourite tee-shirt, the one with a steam engine on the front saying *Getting all Steamed up in Ecclestone.* The souvenir he'd brought home when he was fourteen and gone to the rally with his Uncle Frank. A day Jeffrey will never forget for its gleaming engines, the smell of motors churning, the people, the hotdogs. But mostly it was the whole day, almost four years ago, with Uncle Frank. Just the two of them.

Jeffrey's mum irons his old school shirt; the only shirt he has with a collar. And they find a tie that once belonged to Uncle Frank that would do at a pinch. Jeffrey is happy that Uncle Frank will be with him, in the spirit of his blue and red striped army tie, for his first ever job interview.

The position was advertised in the paper last week. "You could do that," said Jeffrey's mum. She helped him word the application and made sure he included his best school results. And now he has an interview.

He chains his bike to the railings outside an old red brick office building and within minutes finds himself guided down a long brown corridor that smells of burnt cauliflower. Jeffrey tries hard not to count the panels along the walls and is happier once they reach a brightly lit hall.

"Please sit here," he is told.

He joins four people already seated at a long trestle table putting purple triangles in green boxes, and red circles in yellow boxes. Jeffrey joins in and enjoys it immensely.

This is followed by a session to teach him standard responses, a quick photo and he is given his ID badge. And told, along with the others, to start the next day.

They are given two pads of forms, one blue and one pink, a board with a big plastic bulldog clip, and a box of HB pencils, and a little orange notebook. Jeffrey has no trouble working out how to fit all these things into his saddlebag. He doesn't want to jam them in but takes his time and works out how they can all fit, just like his old Perfection game at home.

He pedals home feeling elated, like a man; 'the man of the house' skitters in his mind with each push of the pedal. Through the evening he rubs his forefinger up and down the laminated ID badge, gently stroking the photo of his frowning face, trying to iron out the furrows. "Well," he says to the photo, "you are now a *Market Researcher*." He puffs up his chest in front of his dressing table mirror, "Researcher," he says again.

Jeffrey tries on his parka for his first day of his first job but decides on Uncle Frank's bequeathed pepper-and-salt tweed sports jacket. It is too warm for spring really, but with the id badge clipped to the pocket, he has to admit, it looks very professional.

He eats his 3-minute-boiled-egg-with-soldiers breakfast his mum has proudly placed before him. "A working young man needs something in his stomach," she says, and "have you got a clean handkerchief?" followed by, "make sure you go to the toilet before you leave."

Jeffrey freewheels down Birkenhead Avenue. After all that, his mum hasn't reminded him about his bicycle clips, so his grey trouser bottoms are pushed into his sock tops.

He knows the area he has been allocated only too well, not far from his old school. Jeffrey starts to get that heavy feeling he always got on school mornings, when the closer he got to the school, the heavier the feeling got. Until, more often than not he was sick on the grass verge just outside the gates.

"Those days are over," he tells himself, even though he is a bit queasy. He arrives at Mersey Close, leans his bike against the yellow privet hedge, and knocks on the first door. He waves his ID badge in the face of a tiny bird-like woman who has her hair in curlers and is chewing on nothing. "Good morning," he says, just like they told him to. "I'm a market researcher for Wonderful Stuff, please can I ask you a few questions?"

"Piss off," says the bird-like woman, "I'm sick of you religious freaks."

Jeffrey is perplexed. They told him this could happen and he tries to remember the correct response, smiles as it comes to him, and says," That's quite alright Madam, I will leave the form and collect it next Friday." He hands her a pink (for female) form and makes a note in the little orange notebook. *Lady at number one Mersey Close - left form, call again Friday.*

He knocks on the door of the next house, resisting the temptation to pick at the peeling dark green paint. There is no response, he knocks again with more confidence. The door is flung wide open.

"Hey," says a thuggish looking guy with a pock-marked face and no shirt, "Watcha want? Gerronwithit my breakfast is burning." The thug turns, makes signs with his thumbs at Jeffrey who takes this that he should follow.

Jeffrey pulls his trouser bottoms out of his socks, wipes his feet on the door mat, like they told him, and goes through the littered (with dirty socks and vodka bottles) hallway to the kitchen. The smell of pizza adds to his queasiness. He tries not to gag. The thug makes that he should sit down. Jeffrey knows he is supposed to be polite, no matter what. So he sits, upright, knees together, facing the thug, who has his mouth stuffed so full he cannot speak, and begins his patter, "I am with the Wonderful Stuff..."

The thug motions that he wants to see Jeffrey's Wonderful Stuff stuff. "Prrshow me," he spits; red drool and pizza bits dripping down his bare hairless torso.

Jeffrey produces a blue (for male) form, and passes it through the detritus of pizza triangles, across the table. The thug snorts, drips tomato sauce on it and pushes it back. "You do it for me," he says, "Numb-nut. Numb-nut. Numb-nut."

Jeffrey hears the words. The words that have haunted him since Special Ed at school. He sees the old unrelenting taunting, still there in the thug's eyes, and cowers as pieces of pizza fly across the table. He is determined that he will not go back to being the brunt of this treatment, not now. Not now that he is a man. With a job.

They'd warned him about Rottweilers and loudmouthed men in singlet vests, but they'd said nothing about pizzas or tomato sauce that ran down unshaven chins and dripped on the forms. And nothing about bullies from his old school.

Jeffrey pedals hard up Birkenhead Avenue. The highly polished spokes are just a blur. His tweed jacket is soaked in sweat. Without bicycle clips, his trouser bottoms are fraying, but he needs to hurry and wants tell them that people are maniacs and, in any case, he can't complete their forms because the purple and red shapes are missing.

But at the top of the hill, he stops. He sees the shapes of the town below him. They are not purple or red. He sees clearly the quadrant that is his. And he knows it is his to conquer. He pulls out the little orange notebook and writes: *Man at number three Mersey Close uncooperative. Left damaged form.*

5. Indigo Sweetwater

The storm was forecast to rage for days. There was plenty of warning by officials, but Indigo Sweetwater knew, long before the scientists and the hurricane centre, that this would be a big one. She knew when it would peak too. She was ready, but not being one to panic, took her time, and after a week, gave in to the rising river. She left her trailer in the forest, followed the narrow path alongside the river until she reached the town and joined the rest of the community in the high school gym, the storm shelter.

There was a party atmosphere. It reminded her of the pow-wows of her youth when people sang about their lives, when there was laughter and the sharing of food and drink. And when stories were told. She remembered all of them in detail and often wondered about writing them down. 'One day,' she told herself, 'one day.' In the storm shelter, makeshift beds were put up in rows by the military. Indigo wondered if this was how Residential School was. She knew about the children being taken from their tribes by government officials and being placed in the boarding schools where they were taught to forget their native cultures. She heard how badly they were treated and was glad those days were over; that time now was spent in healing the old wounds.

The winds reached 120 kms per hour on the final night.

By dawn, the rain stopped and people walked out of the high school gym to get a feel for the conditions. Indigo breathed deeply and nodded. "It's okay now, it's over," she told the people around her.

The official announcement came half an hour later: "You can go home, or at least, go see if you still have a home. Buses are laid on for you if you need them."

Most of the town's residents gathered their few possessions and pets and climbed into the old yellow school buses or hitched rides with neighbours. Not Indigo, she looked for her regular trail, the narrow path alongside the river.

She had her few belongings. She still wore the jeans and black tee-shirt she'd had on when she'd left her home. She'd slept in them every night and couldn't wait to change into fresh clothes. In hand-beaded moccasins, she picked her way between fallen trees, searching for her well-worn path. The path of her ancestors.

The land was changed—like entering a new world. Indigo recognised very little. Only the large granite rocks remained; trees lay fallen like pick-up sticks, their monstrous roots now vertical, heavy with earth and moss, tentacles reaching high into the grey sky like monsters from a movie.

'This is worse than I thought,' she muttered, climbing over the trees, cursing the thorns. Birds heralded her progress. Crows cawed like tuneless trombones, blue jays laughed like wicked crones, but the chickadees and chipmunks chirruped Indigo along her way, giving her assurance.

It took three hours of stumbling and picking through forest debris before Indigo reached the clearing where her trailer once stood. She'd had very little to start with. Now she could see she had nothing. Her walls lay flat on the ground. Fragments of furniture littered the area. Her treasured hand-beaded wall hanging—one her grandmother had given her—draped from a huckleberry bush. For the first time, Indigo's eyes welled with tears.

With her hands, she scooped fresh clear water from the rapid river, splashed her face, then drank greedily. Compared to the bottled water that she'd been given in the shelter this water was as sweet as ever. The pure taste told her not everything was lost.

She sat on a fallen tree trunk, looked around at the devastation and tried to gather her thoughts. She knew what her mother and her grandmother would have done in these circumstances. Indigo stood and looked with a new set of eyes. She wandered, looking at the giant tree roots, feeling them, marvelling at their enormity, at their intricacies, and how much of nature was normally unseen. She stepped through the forest, getting to know the new landscape, plucking the ripe blackberries that had survived the storm, gathering the chanterelle mushrooms that flourished beneath the young pines that were still standing. 'I'll need to set a rabbit snare, must have something to compliment the mushrooms,' she told herself. Indigo rubbed the wild thyme through her fingers. She knew, at that moment, that she would survive.

She arrived at the biggest of the fallen trees, its roots spiralling high above some of the other treetops. 'Grandfather's tree. I am so sorry,' she cried. This was the maple he had planted when a young boy, the tree he always sat beneath to sort out problems in his mind, and to talk with Indigo in the few years he'd had with her before his death. She gently stroked the fallen tree and picked at the moss and roots as a way to help her through the devastation. She cleaned the roots out of respect for the giant living thing that was now dying, wondering if there was something from the tree she could plant, someway it could live on. She collected the winged seed and looked for small shoots to plant, gently picking through.

Then Indigo stopped. She felt something unnatural. It was a tin box. Buried under the giant maple, and now uprooted. She continued to pull at the earth and roots until the box was freed. It was not large, about the size of the salmon that leapt in the river. Indigo carried it back to her fallen tree trunk. It was not difficult to open, although locked, the hinges were rusted and the lid came away without effort.

The contents of the box were wrapped in cloth and parchment. There were papers, deeds, and it became quite clear, the land as far as the ridge was hers. That included the river and the mine. The gold in the box with the deed showed the quality of the mine. Indigo thought back to her grandmother's saying, 'Nature will always hold the answer.'

Indigo asked herself, was this purely coincidence, or was the storm supposed to be? Whatever it was, she knew her problems were solved.

Head held high, she walked back to the river she now knew carried her name, Sweetwater. She acknowledged the riches it held.

6. Life's Trappings

Before now, you'd never given traps too much thought. You'd watch lobster traps being brought ashore at the end of the season. You'd see chins slobbering with garlic butter. Wild greedy eyes devouring that mama lobster who was forced against her will to leave behind her little ones because they were 'too small' to be caught this season.

Then you can't forget poor wee Angus, your delicate tabby rescue kitten, you found him with a snare tight, so very tight, around his fragile neck. Gone from this world before he'd caught his first mouse or rat.

Talking of rats and traps. You thought, recently, you had elephants in the attic; well given the thunderous patterings, who wouldn't? So you set a rat trap above the aptly named trap door. And it was with much sadness after three days you found an ermine, too beautiful for words, caught by his slender neck. You didn't offer the much-sought-after pelt on e-bay for dollars—instead you buried him with a dignified ceremony (you humming something by Bach) under the apple tree alongside your wee Angus.

The Bach thing reminds you of how the organist thumped out Air on a G String as you stepped in time down the aisle of St Mark's in 1964. Wearing ivory brocade with lilies of the valley pinning down a veil of silk netting, you didn't feel one bit trapped. In fact the opposite, this was your ticket to freedom. Wasn't it?

It took thirty years for you to understand what that netting symbolised. How it enshrouded you with constraints and limitations. You felt 'caught'.

*

Swim free little lobsters while you can. Stay close to home little kitties and enjoy your mousing this side of the hunting limits. And you beautiful weasels that will become exotic ermine, if you must insist on making your winter homes in attics, please tiptoe gently at night.

And for you brides-to-be, beware the snare of silk netting.

7. Joe's Trip to the Library

"I'll be okay, thank you," Joe says, with a smile. He's packed according to his routine list. Emergency contact number: check. Torch: check. Library card: check. Travel card: check. Water bottle: check. Peppermints: check.

He shuffles down the front garden path, brushing his hand along the pink geraniums. The gate squeaks. He wishes he'd oiled it yesterday. Joe almost stops and goes back for the oil can. But no, he carries on to the bus stop.

*

Imelda worries from the moment the gate squeaks shut. As Joe disappears around the corner into Penzance Avenue, she's pretty sure he'll get himself lost again. She's written down step-by-step instructions: Number 11 bus to the town centre. Left and left again to the library. Railway books are under 'transport—aisle 14'. On leaving library turn right and right again for the bus stop. Number 12 bus to Penzance Avenue. Turn left for home.

She makes herself a pot of tea at 4 o'clock. Joe should be home by now. She slowly dunks her digestive biscuit but, with her preoccupation for Joe's safety, it disintegrates and sinks to the bottom of her Royal Albert. Imelda pushes aside the net curtains, watching for him, her ears pricked for the squeaky gate.

*

Joe sits at the train station. He knows it isn't the library. He knows that he didn't turn left and left again. This is so much better, he tells himself, breathing in that railway smell. Hunting through his backpack for Imelda's instructions, he feels the water bottle and hears the crackle of the bag of peppermints. He sucks on a peppermint as the express for Paddington roars through. He knows it is the 4.30. He knows it arrives at Paddington at 5.12. He knows the next train through will be the 4.34 slow train to Oxford. He also knows he will be late for tea. At his feet are tickets and travel brochures passengers have thrown down. Being a stickler for tidiness, for the environment, and for very smart railway stations, Joe collects them all and stacks them neatly on the bench beside him.

This is my place, he tells himself again. With the excitement of rumbling whooshing noises and the oily diesel smells, he wonders if The Cornishman will come through — he's seen pictures of it in library books. And then, as if he'd waved a magic wand a train pulls in. Penzance it says on the front of the engine.

Joe boards the train with a smile. He can still smell Imelda's pink geraniums on his hands and wants to tell her, "I'll be okay thank you."

8. Tick Tock

"Too little, too late." they said.

"If only we'd known," they said.

"Is there nothing more we can do?"

"To save ourselves and the planet too? Or do we have to sacrifice one now? For the other?"

Marianne remembers how it was years before. When in the late spring everyone burned the grass. Expansive fields of grass, dead and pale as corn from the winter's ravages. Acres of the stuff. Miles of it.

Communities stood with spades and forks and water hoses lest the grass fires got out of hand. And when it was all done, in the early summer new good vibrant grass grew over the scorched earth. Cattle loved it.

Cucumbers loved it too. There was always an abundance for pickling later. In the fall.

This was before committees in cities sat around tables and deemed it wrong to burn. "Think of the ozone," they said, without explanation.

"Consider the black holes," they said, sounding so expert.

"We have to protect the planet," they yelled across gleaming mahogany boardroom tables. With papers before them. Alongside plastic water bottles. Tablets in one hand. Cellphones in the other. Brief cases at their feet.

And so the country folk stopped their spring rituals. Old men chuntered, but didn't fancy the fines, or going to jail either

Wild animals continued to cross borders as they'd done for centuries. Along with their passengers who'd never done any harm.

Before now.

"Ticks will rule the world," says Marianne over breakfast. "They'll destroy us all. With these obscure antibiotic-resistant diseases they carry. Just look at Glenda and Frank down the road. Gone within three months of being bitten by those black-legged deer ticks. 'It's nothing, 'Frank had said, 'just a bite. 'apparently. He dabbed it with whisky. Knowing going to the doctor was not worth it now. The tell-tale bullseye mark around the bite appeared the next day. Frank just dabbed on more whisky. And then to Glenda's bullseyes too."

"And how long is it now since we lost Rufus? Four years since there've been any dogs or cats or rabbits... The pharmaceutical companies flogged those pet tick meds right up until last year was it? Or was it the year before, yes 2013, that was it. And do you remember what a dog's bark sounds like? Or a cat's purr?"

"And just look at us all, dressed in white from tip to toe just so we can spot the little bastards. Jim in the village was fined $500 for wearing blue last week. Against the law. A white population. No colour left in this world—apart from jewelled green grass sparkling with white ticks—because yes, they've got the intelligence to do that too."

"Never mind the lunatic politicians. Never mind terrorism. The ticks are the terrorists. Then they'll have this beautiful planet to themselves." Marianne continues without stopping for breath.

Pete knows he'll have to calm her down. He knows the scientists are now helpless to develop a solution to the epidemic of the diseases carried by the seemingly insignificant insect. Almost too tiny for the naked eye to spot. The size of a poppy seed.

The population wasn't warned. The ticks knew about antibiotics. They were warned.

Pete brings in the shopping from the truck. Just a small bag now, he knows the planet will win, the ticks will win. He's bought just enough for their last supper. He suspects the politicians knew what they were doing when they legalized cannabis. To create a docile population. He knows the dosage he and Marianne will need this night to overcome the blinding headaches, the burning fevers, the joint agony, the muscle loss. To just let go the fight.

In the evening, Pete and Marianne will dress in their favourite bright and colourful clothes from the old days: scarlets and fuchsias, purples and marigold oranges. They will lie together on the tick-laden grassy bank behind their home, the grass they'd had to avoid for years. They will watch the sky turn from blue to violet and they'll drift into oblivion.

9. The Kid, the Cat-girl, the Green Bicycle, and the Chameleon

Beyond the cracked sidewalk, and the telephone pole with layers of flyers in a rainbow of colours, and the patch of dry brown grass stood a ten-foot-high concrete block wall, caked with dozens of coats of paint. There was a small shrine at its foot, with burnt out puddled candles and dead flowers and a few soggy once-yellow teddy bears. One word of graffiti filled the wall, expertly done, red letters on a gold background: *Rejoice!*

Tony stood before the shrine. "Git 'er cleaned up, Kid," was the order barked at him that sultry morning. Community Service was a breeze, or so Tony thought. Picking up old Tim Horton's* cups was the best bit. He found so many 'roll up the rims'** not even rolled up, his heartbeat like that pop punk drummer, Chuck Commeau (or at least that's what Tony thought his name was), wondering if he'd won a Jeep. Or at least a Boston Creme donut. (*Tim Horton's - is a Canadian donut franchise - **' roll up the rim' is an annual draw with possible prizes printed under the rim of the paper cup).

He kicked at nothing. He pulled on a pair of ripped, baby-blue rubber gloves and dipped his hands into the bucket of murky water. He dragged out the scrub brush, leaving a trail of brown sludge across the worms of candle wicks, the shrivelled pink (turning brown) carnations, across the sad drowned teddy bears and up the wall to the red writing. Waiting for the liquid to run down his arms as always. Waiting to feel it fill up his arm pits. Waiting to feel. One of the teddy bears didn't look too bad. That one wasn't yellow, it was pink. With shiny black eyes and a grin. Small enough to stuff in his pocket. He looked up at the word: *Rejoice!* And decided not to scrub it off.

A couple of blocks away, on the striped-mown lawn behind her executive double-fronted mock-Georgian residence, in a white bikini, lounged Amethyst Barclay. The orange and cream azaleas bordering the lawn were in full bloom and she considered, for a very brief moment, if she should cut them for vases for her foyer, for all the bathrooms, for the dining room, in fact throughout the house. But the midday sun was far too tempting. She sipped on a vodka cocktail, closed her eyes and dreamed of Kevin and his muscles.

The Community Service boss yelled, "Dinner break, Kid," at Tony. The mud from the scrubbing had spread from Tony's arms and armpits to his red plaid thrift shop shirt and pull up jeans. He joined 'the boss' in the Community Service green truck. Some kids dragged themselves over. Others didn't bother. Only a couple had food with them. But bananas and water bottles were still handed round. Tony scraped off the remaining flesh from inside his banana skins with his Bugs Bunny front teeth. A chorus of eeew and gagging ensued. But Tony shrugged, "Best bit," he told them, reaching for theirs before they hit the garbage can.

Amethyst Barclay stirred herself. It was 2.15 and time to take the Volvo two blocks away to pick up her daughter from playgroup. Zoe-Giselle had only started at the exclusive childcare facility last month. Just an hour on a Wednesday. "Hardly worth getting her dressed and in the car for just an hour," Amethyst had muttered to the child's absentee father. But he'd insisted, "Part of parenting," he'd said. Firmly.

Zoe-Giselle was advanced for her age. She knew things. She listened. She watched. She recounted these things in her own made-up songs. She wore little round pink eyeglasses which made her look very smart. Either that, or a child with learning difficulties. They most certainly didn't make her look a pretty little girl, in spite of her tangled curls and pink hair ribbons. Not even her fancy boutique cotton dresses in pastel shades with elaborate embroidered smocked bodices could do that. But for playgroup that afternoon, much to her mother's irritation, she'd dressed herself in a pink fluffy cat suit.

Tony stopped on his way back to his squat. He'd seen the 'Help Wanted' notice in the window of the pizzeria. Tony knew he'd have to clean himself up before enquiring further. The thought of a proper job gave him a buzz. The thought that they might give him free pizza too was very attractive. Better than free Boston Cremes from Tim Horton's, that's for sure. Plus, the thought that his mother might be proud of him, was important too. "Rejoice..." he hummed, remembering the graffiti on the wall, remembering his mother singing at church.

There was a bright emerald green bicycle leaning against the pizza place's front window. Tony ran his hands over the curved handlebars. A creature sat on the cross bar, a bright green creature looking like a dragon. A yell from inside the pizza place told him to get his hands off. It felt like an electric shock to Tony who still couldn't get used to being yelled at, something his mother never needed to do.

"Geez, I'm sorry," said Tony. "But there's a dragon..." He'd once seen something on the TV about dragons. That was when he lived with his mom. Before he took off to find an independent life. Before he began making mistakes and getting into trouble. Before he was dragged into court for stealing. For stealing he hadn't done. For protecting his new street friends.

"Do you want a job, Kid?" Yelled the voice. "If so, get yer ass in here, we've got deliveries to go out. Hope you can ride a bike." Tony straightened up, brushed off as much mud as he could. Hoped it wouldn't be noticed. Removed his ball cap. Held his head high and walked into the pizzeria.

He was given an address he'd never heard of. The pizza was in a large red zippered plastic case. The green bike had a tray for the pizza case to fit. "Come straight back here and we'll see about hiring ya." Tony took the red hat offered to him, hopped on the bike, kicked off, and pedalled for all he was worth, hoping the pizza would still be hot by the time he'd found the house. "Hang on little dragon," he whispered.

Amethyst Barclay opened the door to a kid half covered in mud holding out a pizza box. "Rejoice. Delivery," the kid said with a crooked smile. He had white teeth between his muddy lips. Mahogany black hair poked out from under his red Delightful Pizza ball cap. It wasn't Kevin, the guy she'd been waiting for, the guy who normally delivered pizza and more…this was just a kid. A kid with the weirdest sense of humour.

"You'd better come in Pizza Kid," said the glamorous woman at the door of the fancy house. He kicked off his muddy sneakers and tip-toed in bare calloused feet to the gleaming black and stainless-steel kitchen. There was no smell of cooking. Or food of any kind. And he wondered why folks had kitchens if they were going to order take-out pizza. He imagined how over-the-moon his mom would've been in such a palace. How she would cook him stews and meatballs and apple pies. His mouth watered.

Sitting on a bar stool at the fancy kitchen island Tony felt he might be in heaven. He was given a slice of the pizza he'd delivered. "Thank you," he said, "rejoi…" but stopped when he saw the glamorous woman raise her eyebrows. Being called Pizza Kid made him feel official. There was a little girl, dressed in a pink fluffy cat outfit, sitting at the kitchen island too, Gently picking off the olives and placing them in a circle around her plate. He knew he should be getting back to the pizza place if he wanted the job. If he wanted to be paid. If he wanted free pizza. But wasn't this just as good? he asked himself. On top of that he had a green bike with a dragon. And a litre bottle of soda pop. The woman opened a bottle of wine.

Tony had never seen a woman drink so much. He needed to leave, so pulled on his sneakers. He didn't look back to see if the woman was watching. She had drunk more than one bottle of wine. He saw the top of her yellow hair poking up on the top of the couch. He was all set to go back to see about the job when the little pink fluffy cat said, "Take me wiv you. Please. I won't make a sound. I'll be good as a gold bar. Meeow-meeow." He stuffed the bits of the left-over pizza in a paper bag to take with him.

Tony was just a kid himself, but a good kid deep down, everyone used to say that. He could see the little cat-girl could be in danger if he left her behind. How the knives were too close to her level. How the knobs on the stove were within reach. His imagination told him that the right thing to do was to help her. "C'mon then," he said. "But you'll have to ride the bike with me. What's yer name?"

43

"Rainbow, and I like you, ok. Meeow," she half-mewed, half-whispered, lining the front delivery basket with a blanket from the back of one of her mother's armchairs. Tony helped her climb in and get comfortable. He set the green dragon on her lap. "Look at the pretty colours," said the cat-girl. "They match my fluffy coat. Pretty stripes in pink. Can I call you Rainbow? Like me?"

As they bowled along the backstreets, Tony saw the little cat-girl had nodded off in the front tray of the bike. He thought about her smartness. How she knew many things. How she probably knew what *rejoice* really meant. How she probably knew the tune too. All this in the few moments they'd sat together at the island eating pizza. The pink pointy ears on her hat hung by threads. If he took his hands from the handlebars, well, you know what might happen, so he watched the cat-girl, her pink cheeks, her pink fluffy hat, and the fragility of it all. Especially the ears as they finally gave in to the wind and took off to a life of their own among the debris in the roadside gutter. He thought of her as a weak, neglected kitten, with no mama kitten to feed or care for her. It was at this point Tony decided being a Pizza Kid was not for him. Taking care of kittens was more his bag. He took a detour to a place he knew. His old garage hideout. His safe place. The place where he was able to be himself, to meditate, to think, to hum, to—yes—rejoice. To sort out the problems with the world immediately around him.

When the ride ended, she was lifted again. The kid slid her body onto a soft pile of clothing among the boxes in the garage. He pulled an old coat over the top, creating a cave that emanated the sweetness of old ladies who frequently powdered themselves—a light rose motif that played ironically well in the deep recesses of Rainbow's ancestral brain. The pizza kid lifted her head to help her lap water from a hubcap. He broke bits of pepperoni and crust into bite-sized pieces and left them where her tongue could reach them.

Much later, she heard him practicing his orations like songs. Like monks chanting in the distance, they were a comfort.

Back on Amethyst's fancy leather couch, a vomit bucket had been placed on the floor at her head end. A man talked on the phone, "That's right, a little girl with glasses. No, no, I don't know what she was wearing. My wife says probably a pink fluffy suit. I know, I know there's a heatwave. There is a pizza box here. That's all I know. Her mother is passed out drunk." Bradley Barclay ran his hands through his hair. "Where did I go wrong?" He asked his phone.

The search for Zoe-Giselle was underway. Six cops raided the pizza joint. The Barclays were big shots in the city. All the stops were being pulled out. The pizzeria's owner stuttered and stumbled and muttered about a green bike and a very muddy delivery kid (with no name) and where was his money for the pizza? And more importantly, where in the hell was his expensive chameleon?

In the incident room pictures of the little girl, her drunken mother, the fancy home, a Volvo, pizzas, a pink fluffy suit, and magazine cut-outs of green bicycles—were stuck to a board with magnets. There was no picture of a muddy kid. Cops made notes in their notepads. The conclusion was that they should search for a green bicycle first. And muddy kids second.

Rainbow looked at Tony. Then at the food in the hubcap, "I'm not eating that shit," she said, sounding more like a forty-something woman with a headache. "What do you think I am, a cat or something?" She looked up at him then, sucked in her pink cheeks showing her dimples. "Let me make something then, do you have a toaster? Or a microwave, yes a microwave would be good."

But Tony had none of these and in any case, there was no power in the disused garage. The only option was for him to go in search of proper food for this sweet kitten who talked like a little-big girl. "What kind of thing would you like then? You know, you were the one who wanted to come with me, I didn't make you." He reached into his pocket for the tiny pink teddy bear he'd picked up at the job site. The little-big cat-girl cradled it like a baby.

The Community Service boss was on the phone to the office, "That kid Tony didn't show up this morning," he said. "Can someone track him down, I thought he was doing really well, but he's a bit of a worry, I don't know if he has a real home or anything." He put the phone in his pocket and turned to the rest of the Community Service kids. "OK then," he said, "c'mon guys, who knows where Tony lives?"

Bradley Barclay, Zoe-Giselle's father, needed to leave town for a critical meeting of financial minds. He was torn between the fact that his little daughter had been kidnapped, and the amount of money he could make if he flew to Singapore at 7 pm. And that money would pay whatever ransom the kidnapper demanded. He tried to talk to his wife, Amethyst. "Please, Honey, you must remember." He tried with all his might not to get angry, not to punch her in her over-made-up face with its running black mascara, not to pull her bedraggled once-coiffed hair out. "Just think back," he said. "The pizza? Tell me again. The pizza."

Amethyst Barclay looked up at the gorgeous hunk of a man before her. At his big brown eyes that once melted her with a glance. At the flop of dark hair shining from his morning Head & Shoulders. At his hands with that sprinkling of dark hairs along the backs of his fingers and she wondered just where it had all gone wrong. Why did she order pizzas so that she could have a good time for twenty minutes with a delivery guy? And why hadn't the usual guy turned up yesterday? And why was this hunk before her being so nice for a change?

Tony tried to come to a decision that night—should he: 1. take the little/big cat/girl home to her neglectful drunken mother, or 2. take her to the police station? He knew that if he did the latter he'd be in even bigger trouble than he was already and that Community Service would be a memory of paradise compared with what could lay ahead. He wondered if his mother would know what would be best and what her advice would be.

Maria woke to the rattle of stones on her bedroom window. She plunged her swollen feet into her bedroom slippers, pulled her midnight blue bathrobe around her and went to peep out of the window. "Oh my God, Tony, where've ya bin? I've bin worried sick. Stay right there, I'll be right down." She scooted down the wooden staircase on her bum, like a nine-year-old trying out a sled for the first time. It was her way of avoiding nasty falls, she'd had far too many of them.

There, on the door stoop, stood Tony. He had a green bicycle and a little girl in a pink fluffy cat suit. He also had a dragon on his shoulder. "Ma," he said, "I didn't know what to do. I couldn't leave her, I worried she'd get hurt." He briefly shrugged at the green bicycle. He rolled his eyes at the chameleon who had climbed on to Maria's bathrobe and turned midnight blue. And then he closed his eyes as if in prayer, knowing his mother couldn't refuse her help.

With no admonishment for the son she loved, Maria wrapped one arm about him, the other around little girl and the chameleon—but not the green bicycle—that was propped against the rusting chain-link fence. "Get in quick," she said, "I know it's summer, but it can't be that warm out there at this time of night. Does the critter have to come in too?" She looked at the chameleon as if it was about to bite a chunk out of her arm. Then laughed, "Of course he can. What's his name?"

"Her name's Rainbow, like mine," piped the girl. "She won't hurt you, she's cute. A girl not a boy by the way." The small girl's words came from her mouth like words from a TV newscaster. Tony released her from his arms. In the kitchenette she leant against the sink, as if it was her natural habitat.

Maria made them crispy bacon and hash browns. She tossed sunny-side-up fried eggs on top. And cut big hunks of bread from the loaf she'd made that day. No butter. Tony smelled the familiar aroma of the bacon frying. He smiled at the girl, "We'll be okay here. We can find somewhere else tomorrow." He smiled at his mother, "I didn't know where to bring her. What do you think we should do Ma?"

"Tell me what happened," said Maria. "Right from the beginning, but not until we have this little one settled to sleep." With a pillow and a blanket, Rainbow/Zoe-Giselle was placed, gently on the threadbare couch. She immediately fell asleep, her rosebud mouth slightly open, little bubbles formed as she breathed deeper and, eventually Maria and Tony could see she was in a deep sleep, the kind of sleep unique to the young and the brave. "Talk to me, Son," Maria said. "Let us work this through together. But first we will say our little prayer, the one for troubled times. *Rejoice in the Lord...* Tony slowly closed his eyes and put his hands together.

Patrol cars were sent to drive slowly up and down all the streets in town. They were told to follow the grid system and look for a green bicycle. Nothing more, just a green bicycle. And if they found it to call it in and drive on a block before stopping. Guy and Ed were partners in car 44. They began their cruise at 2 am. "Don't call it the graveyard shift for nothing," said Guy. "So if you wanna snooze while I drive, that's fine. I'll be able to spot a friggin' bike, especially a green one."

"Wassat?" Yelled Ed, waking up from a super dream about giant banana split. "Look, over by the side if the road, in the gutter." Guy stopped the patrol car with a scream of brakes and backed up. Ed hopped out, 'S'nuttin',' he said, "A couple of pink fluffy ears, must be left over from Hallowe'en or some such thing." He threw them back in the gutter under a yellow sign that said, '$50 fine for littering.'

Ed and Guy finished their shift at 8 am. They hadn't seen a green bike. Loads of bikes, but in the dark it was hard to see the colour. And under street lights they all looked purple to

Ed, but then again Ed was just a tad colour blind, it seemed a miracle that he passed the test for the police force, but he did well in math and Spanish, so he sailed in. They made out their report that there were no sightings and sat down for breakfast in the cafeteria with their colleagues. "There's been a reward offered," they heard in the noisy chatter, and looked at each other, questioning whether police officers could qualify, but then looked down again at their pancakes, knowing the answer.

The Barclays had one of their enormous rows. More enormous than normal. "Just don't go," Amethyst said to Bradley. He stood in their marble foyer, looking at the bleakness of his home, devoid of colour, devoid of personality, devoid of character of any kind. Devoid of love. His suitcase was packed. His tablet was in his briefcase. His mobile phone in his pocket. "If you go now, we may never find her. Why do you have to go?"

Bradley Barclay looked at his wife, the mother of his precious daughter, the woman who neglected to care for her, for their home, and for him, and he hadn't got time to work out where and when it all went wrong. But wrong is where they were at, at that moment in time. Wrong. And he dearly wanted to put things right. If not for his family, then at least for his daughter. Before him stood a bedraggled wretch of a woman. A woman who once was beautiful, once had shiny fair hair, once had sparkling blue eyes, and a bounce in her step and her voice. Now it was as if all the energy had drained from her. And it was at this point that Bradley Barclay changed his mind.

"We must take the little girl home," said Maria to her son who was still on the well-worn Lazy-Boy where he had slept. "The only way is for you to do the right thing." She looked at Tony and saw the child she once cradled in her arms when things went wrong, when she kissed his grazed elbows or knees, when she cuddled him into bed at night after reading a story. She looked at him again and saw a confused but kind young man and she knew that all he'd done had been done out of kindness. "Get dressed," she said to him. "Get dressed and take the bike back. I will look after the little one." She watched the chameleon wander across the kitchen table, turning yellow as it brushed against the pottery milk jug. "Take the dragon too, it is where she belongs."

Tony wove through back alleys and pedestrianised roads to the pizzeria. The chameleon perched happily in the pizza tray, returning to her normal green. "I'll be sorry to leave you," Tony said, "but it is where you live." The chameleon closed then opened one eye in acknowledgement. Tony nodded back as he tip-toed the bike the last few feet to the back entrance of the pizzeria and leaned it, softly, against the wall. "Have a nice life," he whispered. Whether to the bike or to the chameleon, an onlooker could not be sure

The Community Service boss jumped into the truck and prepared to pick up the kids for the days work. He'd had a good breakfast of ham, eggs and beans and he picked his teeth with a toothpick from his supply in his top pocket. He reached across the dash for his gum and that is when he saw the note: *"sorry I missed yesterday, I will try and get to work today, Tony."* He immediately dialled the office before going to pick up the kids.

The Community Service kids were litter picking in the gutters. The boss told them that Tony is not lost but he'll probably turn up today and, as he left a note, will probably not be in too much trouble. The kids sniggered but carried on picking up the crap from the edge of the road. More Tim Horton's* cups, they sniggered some more knowing that Tony always wanted those to see if he'd won a Paris vacation or some such thing. "Whatcha got there, Kid?" The boss looked at the bedraggled pink fluffy triangles and remembered the morning news. Remembered that a kidnapped girl might have worn pink. He called 911. "Stop work kids," yelled the boss. "Don't touch another thing, we may have a clue to the missing girl."

Ed and Guy had volunteered for overtime to help in the search. They pulled up, with flashing blue lights and sirens, to the Community Service kids who stood around the boss's truck eating bananas, fooling around, pulling each other by their jackets, calling 'meeow, meeow,' at the kid who'd found the pink ears. "OK, all stand back," ordered Guy. "Let's see what we have here." He looked at Ed and rolled his eyes, remembering they'd seen these things the night before. "Bag 'em, Ed," he said, "we need to take these to forensics."

Bradley answered his phone. He looked across at his wife, at her swollen face from sobbing, he saw a glimpse of the innocent young woman he first fell in love with. "They've found something," he said. "They've told us to stay here and not to worry." He took her another cup of chamomile tea, something his mother always drank in a crisis. "Tell me," he said. "Tell me everything."

Amethyst dried her eyes and blew her nose. "I need a life," she said. It was probably the most profound statement Bradley had heard from her in years. "I'd like to work." Again he was lost for words. He had thought that the life of luxury he'd provided for his wife was something many women dreamed of. "But first, I'd like to do some courses, qualify for a skill. I'd like work with animals."

The doorbell rang. Amethyst leapt up. All thoughts of college courses out of her mind. Bradley leapt up too, all thoughts of his flights to financial meetings out of his mind, like a breeze across an ocean. He opened the door to find his little daughter standing there with a grin on her face. Beside her was Maria. And Tony. "We've brought your daughter home," said Maria. "My son took her to safety, we just want to make sure that things are safe for her now."

In a flurry of excited jubilation, Zoe-Giselle told her parents about her adventure, how Tony gave her a bike ride with a dragon called Rainbow. How Tony's Mum made them bacon and hash browns and how she slept on their couch dreaming of Mommy and Daddy and how she would be a much better girl when she got home. Bradley and Amethyst immediately saw how happy she was. Saw what good people Maria and Tony were. Amethyst vaguely remembered Tony as the muddy pizza kid—but erased all that pizza stuff from her mind. When the cops arrived, Bradley told them the whole thing was a misunderstanding and that Tony had been hired as a baby-sitter and had taken their daughter to his mother's for the evening. A mix-up in communication. He offered them a big cheque for the police benevolent fund.

Tony and Maria smiled with relief. Tony put his arm around his mother's shoulders. As they began to take their leave, Bradley offered them the reward. Maria vehemently declined and said sorry that she hadn't contacted them earlier. Bradley, knowing they had really helped his family out of a huge hole, and provided them with a wake-up call and a turning point, said, "Let me drive you home, it's the least I can do." But Maria shook her head, unwilling to share their shanty town address. Tony's sad face and worn thrift store clothing gave Bradley clues that this was a loving mother and son with problems.

On impulse he said, "Would you both like jobs? My wife is about to start back at college and we will need someone to be our cook and another to be a babysitter for our precious little girl. I can think of no-one better than both of you. We have a little cottage by the lake where you can live. What do you say?"

Tony knew, given half the chance, Maria would burst into "Rejoice…" at the top of her lungs. But they could save all of that for another day.

10. Bubbling Beetroot

He boils beetroot. You can smell its pungent earthiness from your sickbed upstairs. But you smile. He's in your kitchen boiling beetroot for you because you love it.

He hates it though; you've never learned why. He hates sardines too, you've always thought that was because his Norwegian father ate them all the time, right out of the tin, with oil dribbling down his chin to his rough mariner's shirt. And beyond.

You hear the faint comforting chink of china and cutlery coming from your kitchen. You guess he's emptying the dishwasher.

You remember how, all those years before, he'd taken care of you after the baby came. Being captain of the kitchen was new to him then. Releasing control was new to you too. But you were confined to bed for a week and hated it. How you wanted to be back at the cooker, making meals for him. Washing up. Polishing your wedding present saucepans until you could see your young married face in them.

But he managed that week, with your step-by-step instructions on how to do everything. You remember how he called up, 'Will you be alright? Just popping to the shops, we're out of...'

And how, before he left, you called back down, 'I'll be fine, don't forget to put the potatoes in to soak before you go...'

After you heard the back door click closed, you defied orders and crept down the stairs to take a look at what was going on in your kitchen. To your amusement you saw the potatoes soaking in soapy bubbles.

You crept back upstairs and slipped under the plumped pink quilt and smiled, but you've never forgotten. And you never mentioned it either. Neither did the potatoes taste one bit soapy.

He's doing it again, calling up the stairs, exactly as he'd done fifty years ago, 'Just popping to the shops...'

This time you don't creep down to check on your kitchen, or even the bubbling beetroot. You know it is all in good hands.

11. The Advertisement

Calvin once complained that there were not enough talking parrots in the world. The guys in the bar laughed.

"You fool, Calvin, what do you know about birds?" said Huey.

"You crazy?" said Wes." If not they'll most surely drive you there. With their 'who's a pretty boy then 'and 'knock knock who's there?'" The guys all began knocking on the bar, drumming until Calvin broke into a big smile. He couldn't help himself.

But Calvin kept his own counsel. He didn't like to argue with the guys. After all, they were his buddies, the only people he got to speak with any day of the week. He didn't like to tell them that it wasn't what he meant. There was no use trying to explain that what he really was talking about was old fashioned values, the old ways of living; stuff like weaving and bird watching and seeing ponies jump over hurdles. Even hearing the soothing clacking of knitting needles as a dear lady from his past made him a fawn V-necked pullover for school.

And yes, having the patience to teach a parrot to talk.

Neither did he tell them that somewhere in his checkered, and not always happy, childhood he'd lived with people who had parrots. And that was his happiest, but briefest, childhood interlude. But mostly he'd blocked those times from his memory.

He knew the guys would think he'd gone all fancy, reading his big newspaper with no pictures. They'd soon get him to leave his Harris Tweed hat at home and wear the red sports cap they'd given him. It had the name of a famous football team on it. Calvin wasn't a fan of football. Just thinking about the rough games at a rough school he attended for three months made his mouth go dry. But he wore the red cap to please the guys. He also changed his blue and white striped cotton shirt for a bright red and green flannel plaid. To feel like one of the guys.

On Wednesday he opened up his big newspaper (with no pictures) to browse while he sipped his espresso on his back porch (where no-one would see him). He scanned the world news, the society page to see who was getting married and who divorced, he skimmed the property pages. And there, just before the sports page he saw the advertisement:

Wanted. Good home for two talking parrots: old Henry, and June his partner of a slightly lesser age. They cannot be parted. They have been together all their lives. Phone the number below and we will give you the details.

Calvin couldn't believe it—he felt like this was providence. Not just one, but two parrots. His home would be filled with sound again, with chatter, he'd have someone to talk to. Not just the guys at the bar.

On Thursday he dressed in his Harris Tweed with his blue and white striped cotton shirt and got the old Riley Kestrel out of the garage and drove her gently to the address he'd been given on the phone. In his pocket was the speech he'd typed on his vintage Underwood about why he could give the pair of birds a good home.

Calvin pulled the old fashioned bell chain by the front porch of the Victorian cottage, feeling right at home already. He heard the bell ring like an echo within. And with that his world also began to echo. He touched the peeling paint around the red front door, picking away, seeing a familiar green beneath. He breathed in the scent of climbing sweet peas and remembered a kind lady with pink cheeks and shining blue eyes. And the feel of a soft hand-knitted fawn pullover.

The door opened. She was there. Smiling. "Calvin," she said. "At long last. We've found you."

12. The Return of Minerva

It is a pleasure for Minerva to feel again. To feel the sun. To feel the burn after so much numbness. The blistering heat of the noon Mediterranean sun bores through the pale skin to her frigid bones. She relishes it after the iced deadness that was her mindless winter. The thought of raging sunburn needing a clinic visit doesn't deter her from soaking it up. Or from getting heat stroke? She knows the pleasant warmth she feels now will turn into an agonising pleasure tonight. How she will rage against the cool cotton hotel sheets and long for someone to come. Or not, she'll enjoy it all the same. The pain—proof she is still alive.

"You'll regret it," he whispers, offering sunscreen.

An interruption is not part of her plan at all. She's selected a remote corner of the beach, beyond the sun-loungers, beyond the kiddy rock-pools, beyond the beach walkers with their unleashed hounds. She's chosen a hidden inlet not even visible by drone. Yet here he was. An interruption.

Still, she was raised to be polite. "Too many chemicals," she mutters through closed eyes, half seeing his large hands with scatterings of black hair on the backs of his fingers. Has she ever met anyone with hairy fingers? She tries to remember, even allows herself to drift into other body possibilities.

"We could go for ice cream," he still whispers. "Or a cold beer if you prefer."

She sits. Brushes silver white sand from her bare sunken thighs. Drapes her tangerine silk wrap around her bony now-ripe-pink shoulders. Raises one slender arm, jangling with gold bangles, extending her hand to him, "Minerva," she says, "Minerva Arnold."

***

They are the only people at the beach bar. The tag on the barman's chest identifies him as Aris. He takes up his silver cocktail shaker in anticipation regardless of the hour.

"Sorry to disappoint Aris," she says, "Can I have coffee, please, Greek coffee, with maybe a small Metaxa on the side?"

"So much for the beer," says her companion. He laughs then, showing American white teeth with a glint of gold.

"Sir?" Aris pours salted nuts into a white stoneware bowl and sets it before the giant of a man.

"Yes, please, a beer for me," he says, reaching for the nuts.

Minerva looks at this hairy-backed hand and resists the need to touch. Instead, she picks up her tiny cup. She sips through the familiar scum, tasting the bitter sweetness of her past, wondering, fleetingly, how long she can hang on to this limbo.

"I'm Charley," he no longer whispers.

Minerva trembles as his basso profundo voice reverberates through her. She feels a chill despite the midday heat. She takes more than a sip of brandy and feels the familiar warmth spread to her belly. But Charley? A name she knows? She doesn't want to remember.

***

Minerva naps the afternoon away in her suite, luxuriating in dreams for the first time in her memory. She wakes to the chirruping sounds of cicadas and distant church bells. It is after seven when she steps from her room's hot tub feeling no pain. Not wanting to feel pain, in a way thankful she was saved from the blistering sunburn she'd wished for so hard.

She wears a short ivory silk wrap dress for the evening. With no jewellery other than the same gold bangles. He waits in the hotel lobby in white Bermudas with a Hawaiian shirt of a brilliant cobalt blue emblazoned with scarlet and emerald birds of paradise.

Charley greets her with a peck on her cheek. His Armani cologne hits her memory with such strength she reels in her white slingback sandals. He catches her in an Antonio Banderas tango move. Sets her gently upright, saying, "We'd better eat soon."

Their reserved table on the waterfront, overlooking the harbour, is set with a blue and white checkered tablecloth. Charley orders a meze, and slowly the dishes begin to appear. Warm pita bread cut into triangles. Halloumi with slices of locally grown tomatoes, grilled fish—smaller than sardines with lemon, hummus, tzatziki.

When the dolmades arrive Minerva's mouth waters, "My favourite," she says. Reaching. Taking one between her finger and thumb. Opening her mouth wide to take the stuffed vine leaf. Not worrying about the juices dribbling down her chin. Laughing. And then stopping dead. She understands that laughter has not been part of her life for many months. That food with taste has been absent. And she understands that until this moment she has been somewhere else.

Dozens of cats sit on the low walls that separate their café from others. Two of them come to their table for scraps. Charley makes to get rid of them, but Minerva says, "No, let them come."

They purr like farm tractors around her bare legs and the familiar feel of the soft fur makes her take a deep breath.

65

"I know you," she says.

"You do." It is not a question.

"Where have I been?"

"I will tell you everything," he says. "When you are ready."

13. Pink Capri

The Drugmart advertisement in Saturday's paper caught Beryl's eye. *YesterYear with Yardley* it said, under a grainy picture. The illustration struck a chord: of her and Howard going to the pictures; going to the fair; going on the train to the seaside. Howard was good at deciding where and when to go. Goodness they had such times together.

Beryl never went down the High Street. Even now, she didn't know if she should. In the end she got off the bus before she had chance to change her mind for a fourth, or was it a fifth time? Unused to the roar of the traffic, she wondered about removing her hearing aid. But then again, she wouldn't be able to hear if someone hooted. Would she?

Beryl soon found Drugmart. She wanted to go on Wednesday but couldn't decide whether to wear her red or navy coat. By the time she'd decided, she'd missed the bus and they only ran twice a week. Howard had been gone for over twenty years, but it was still hard without him. He would have said, "Wear the red one, Toots," right off the bat.

The cosmetics department with its glossy consultants lured Beryl in. She pulled off her plastic rain hat and fluffed up her perm, glancing in one of the many mirrors, wondering who the wizened, tired face looking back at her belonged to.

"Can I help you?" the glossy consultant smiled a painted smile.

"Um," said Beryl. "Er, I think it was Pink Capri. The lipstick."

"Pink Capri?" said Miss Glossy. "Let's see what we have in our Retro Range."

Beryl slumped against the counter. She heard faint voices. People's faces were just a blur mingling with shiny articles swimming up and around her: mirrors with old crones, bottles and potions, racks of lipsticks, and the life-sized grainy photo of her and Howard at the fair.

A teary Miss Glossy stood beside Beryl's cordoned-off lifeless body waiting for the paramedics to arrive. She gently tucked a lipstick in Beryl's red coat pocket. "I found your Pink Capri," she said.

14. The City Girl and the Water Diviner

"Is it sweet?" says Trevor.

Prue raises an eyebrow and puts down the blue enamel mug on a flat granite rock. With her embroidered hanky she wipes drips from her no longer dry mouth and says, "Sweet? What do you mean?"

"The water," says Trevor. "What do you taste?"

Again, she looks puzzled. "It's water. Is it supposed to have a taste? It's good though, thank you for finding this spring, I was dying of thirst."

All Trevor knows about Prue is that she wasn't raised in the country. That she doesn't know why porcupines are protected. Doesn't know the health attributes of birch bark. She may know how to make a pretty marvellous chocolate torte—but what's the good of that when you're lost in the woods?

He isn't sure if he should tell her how they used to live. They haven't known each other long. He isn't sure she will understand his simple upbringing. About how they had no electricity, just oil lamps when he was younger. That the toilet was an outhouse in the back yard, a double seater too. And water was hauled up from the well in a bucket.

He sits beside her on the rock, "We always kept a trout in our well when I was a kid, it kept the water clean. And sweet. The well was dug and fed by a spring just like this one. Dad found it."

"Found?"

"Yes he would take a tree branch with a crotch in it and it found the very best place to dig a well. He did it for loads of folks in Indian Point, in exchange for a 40-ouncer of rum."

"Your Dad was a water diviner then?"

"If that's what it's called, well, I'm one too then."

*

They are no longer lost. Refreshed by the spring water they emerge from the woods into the brightness of the shore with the plovers flirting with the breeze, the baying of seals, and the eagles hovering overhead.

"I'll make you supper tonight," announces Prue, "what do you fancy? Porcupine stew followed by chocolate torte?"

Trevor laughs. Only this morning they were like strangers. He takes the hand of the girl who's never tasted water and knows they will have a lot to learn from each other.

15. Daniel

The postcard was the first indication to Margaret and Hugh that Daniel was still alive. They had just about given up all hope. He was fourteen when he went missing. Margaret cried every night for months. She wouldn't leave the house in case there was a phone call, a message or, what she really prayed for, Daniel standing there on the doorstep with his school bag, in his green tee-shirt, his mop of blond hair flopping into his blue eyes.

She couldn't sit still and lived with a duster in her hand, polishing, forever polishing. The house reeked of lavender, but Hugh said nothing. He didn't know how he could help her through the loss of their only son.

He made phone calls and popped into the police station once a week. Posters were put up and Daniel's grainy face appeared on the back of visa statement envelopes: *Have you seen this child?*

But they heard nothing. Until the postcard arrived. "It's a clue," said Margaret, "look, he's given us a clue to where his abductors have taken him."

Hugh looked at the picture of London at nighttime, the lights reflecting on the black waters of the river. "Perhaps you're right," he said. "Is it his writing? The boy always had difficulty with handwriting no matter how much I instilled into him how he needed to do so much better."

"Yes." said Margaret, "I think it must be. But it has been so long." She wiped her face with a lace trimmed hanky and breathed deeply. "We are going, aren't we Hugh? Tomorrow? To find him, and bring him home?"

***

Daniel stood on the riverbank with a group of young men. They could see the middle-aged couple standing, bewildered, looking about them: Margaret in her Laura Ashley pink coat, clutching her old brown handbag. Hugh in his green Barbour jacket, fumbling in his pocket.

"Is that them?" said the tallest of the group.

"Yes," said Daniel.

"OK," said the tall guy, "we're right behind you Danno."

***

Over the months Daniel had told them all about the life he'd left behind. Why he'd run away. They'd seen the scars on his back and in the end, he told them how his father beat him for the slightest thing. Lashing at him with his belt. For not getting A grades, for swearing, for talking at the table, and for wetting his bed.

"The fucking slime-ball, no wonder you wet the bed," they said. "Didn't your mum stop him?"

"The fucking bitch," said Daniel. "Afterwards, she would stuff my mouth with chocolates and make me drink her bitter homemade lemonade. She would kiss me on top of my head and say things like 'there-there, all better now'."

In a year he had grown. The hostel had a gym where he worked out every morning. He learned how to stand up for himself. Now the time had come for him to show his parents what it felt like. Time for Daniel to close that first chapter of his life.

Daniel stood, dressed all in black, tall and strong before Hugh and Margaret now, his head shaved and shining in the lamps that lit the riverbank. His once watery, always ready to weep, eyes, were now hard as steel, and he knew that he had no feelings for these two people. These pathetic cruel people. No feelings at all.

He had a backpack filled to the top with sickly, soft-centred chocolates and bitter lemonade in four large plastic bottles. And he had a belt with a big metal buckle. Daniel also had his gang to back him up.

He wanted to see their fear, wanted to smell their horror. To hear Hugh scream, 'please, no more,' as he lashed his father's disgusting white bare back while the gang held the man down, forcing Margaret to watch. He was ready to see his mother gag on the chocolates as he crammed pound after pound of brown sludge into her sorry lipsticked mouth and pour the grey lemonade, pint after pint into her, letting the bitterness reach her gall. To watch her puke.

And he was ready to say, 'there-there, all better now'.

But Daniel did none of these things. He tossed the backpack on the ground before them, turned, and walked into the black city night with his people.

16. Coming of Age

My sisters give me silken scarves the colours of the setting sun: scarlet, orange, and violet. My mother gives me her well fingered lute so that music will be my companion. Father has crafted me a vessel in clay to carry water, he presents it to me in his strong outstretched arms. Grandfather offers me a muslin-wrapped cheese from his amber-eyed goat.

My grandmother, scooping her long white hair, tying it behind her head in ribbons the colour of the evening sky, gives me her wisdom: "this is a journey you must complete alone. You must not seek help from another, or your destination will not be yours and yours alone."

We smile, and kiss, and wave. But, as I depart on my yellow tuktuk, I feel their sadness and know of their muted wailings and silent pleadings through the throaty puttering of the tuktuk's motor.

In spite of all of this, in my belly, I swell with joy; filled with anticipation to be heading out alone into the world. My destination is the sea beyond the distant blue mountains. From there the boat with the plum-red sails will be waiting. Only a boat, no boatman or boatwoman, as I suppose you have surmised. This boat, made from wood, I will sail myself and circumnavigate my own world. I must find the fresh beginnings that my grandmother promised would be there, in her words, "you will only find them if you seek them." This I understand to be the new life that only exists for me as I turn from a girl to a woman. That no other person would see it as such. A unique life for each and every one of us.

After many sunrises and sunsets, my tuktuk splutters, coughs and will not be coaxed to move. I use all my knowledge and tools to restore the motor, to no avail. I must now decide: stay and wait for another traveller to discover my plight and help me on my way? Or continue, on this journey that is just for me, on foot?

The sun dips behind the mountains, casting shadows as long as monkeys' tails between the reeds. Sipping from my father's clay vessel, I taste the cool liquid's purity of life and certainty. A morsel of Grandfather's salty cheese on my tongue gives me strength. I wind my sisters' scarves around my body for protection.

I pick up my mother's lute and sing the song of my ancestors:

'the walk will be long but my feet are young
my eyes are tired but the view is sweet
my bed is hard but my limbs now float
my voice is soft but I know you can hear'

From the distant hills comes a response:
'I hear you daughter, granddaughter, sister
close your tired eyes and sleep
drift with your dreams and you will sail
away to your destination.'

17. Not Hockney

He stands on my doorstep with his cart of tools. I see no vehicle, no indication that he travelled here using a normal route. We live in a remote part of the province, most folks come by mule. And they bring gifts. Always.

"I have come with a solution to your calescent problem," he says through his unshaved bespectacled face.

I'd heard this before, do you remember? The strange, bearded guy with the backpack, cradling the French loaf, who wanted to solve my problems—'heal your calescent aggression'—those were his very words. How I told him to eff off and not come onto my property again. Surely you remember that day; I offloaded my worries to you that night over the phone. How I felt guilty swearing at a chap who looked like Jesus.

But this man is different. He looks like David once looked. Pale skin, pale hair, pale stubble, vintage glasses over his watered-silk china-blue eyes. That was before he became famous and moved to California.

I'm not uneasy so I invite him in.

Over breakfast the next sizzling morning he says, "The solution to your overheating is in my hands, you just have to give me permission."

I am enthralled. No palpitations of concern, no worrying that I should dial 911, or—God forbid—call my mother. No, I'm happy for him to be here.

At the end of the second week of drought and my dying garden, after he has assembled his equipment, filled the cartridges with colours, sprayed outlines on the dead lawns (partly over the now-brown tennis court—but I don't care, which is strange for me not to rant and rave and ask what the hell he thinks he's doing).

No, I let him have his head. Machines whirr, giant motherboards are erected around the perimeter of my property, colours fly. Many colours—bright vibrant primaries. Colours I've never before seen. I am mesmerized and have an unreal feeling that my life will change.

I wake early the next day—the skies are tinged with violet and apricot and I step over to my balcony as if on air. Looking down to the lawns below I see now what he has done.

My stranger has painted me an enormous Grecian pool. For swimming, for dreaming, for cooling when another day forges on towards its oppressive heat. It is real. I can touch it. Step down into the cool clear turquoise waters. Push off from the shallow end towards the deep depths of blue luxury.

He has gone. Was he ever here?

18. Stiff as Boards

The line of wash crackles in the freezing salt wind. "Stiff as boards," Ma says as she unpins the ice encrusted flannel shirts, letting them fall like planks of cedar into the old tin bath she uses as a laundry basket.

How her fingers don't freeze to its metal handles as she hauls it back across the frozen waste that is our lawn in summer, I'll never know. But in she comes, cheeks the rosiness of the huckleberry pasture in the fall, lips as blue as Da's old coveralls, kicking the kitchen door behind her with her booted foot. She plonks the old tin bath on the floor and repeats herself, "Stiff as boards."

"Just smell the sea." She grins, "smell Da's ole shirt, isn't that just the smell of The Narrows?"

Then she thrusts the 'stiff as boards' clothes under our noses and we, as we know we must, smell. With loud sniffs to please her. Nicky snorts, he sniffs so well. Benny laughs at him. A broad laugh showing all his teeth; looking more like Da every day.

Then we sit around the table while Freda, good and steady Freda, butters the mountain of hot tea biscuits she's taken from the oven just moments ago. Arms reach, as they have done since we were little kids, in competition to reach the platter first. To grab the hot biscuits and cram them in our mouths before the butter melts. Before it trickles down our chins.

Freda smiles and pours steaming tea from the big brown betty into our blue enamel mugs that all say 'Admiral' on the side.

Da won them in a dory race years ago. Back and forth across the gut, ten times. Middle of summer. Arms muscle-bulging. Face redder than the rosy knobs out on the island. Sweat pouring down his bare back like Niagara Falls. Or at least like the pictures I've seen of the falls in last year's calendar. The day he won was a day for celebration. And he came home with the box of mugs, giving one to each of us four kids and Ma. "Well," he said, "I can only drink out of one at a time, cannot I?" And with that he turned to the jug of screech and poured himself a healthy dose, downing it in one before collapsing with exhaustion on the old swing chair on the stoop.

I can see him now, and I know Ma sees him every day too. We miss the old guy. Drunk or sober, we miss him. That's why we all still wear his shirts to this day. So we can feel him close, remember the good days, and forget the day he went out on the scallop dragger to the George's Bank. It was the 30th of January. The day it went down. Fourteen hours out so heavy with ice it just sank with all five crew. Including Da.

"Come on now Callie, let's not sit here dreaming. Help me give this lot a shake out so we can fold 'em," says Ma.

I get up from the table and as I shake and fold the frozen wash, I smell the sea. And Da.

19. The Ballad of Jock McCoy

In his head he is exotic; a flamboyant fellow with swirling purple silk coattails over his red and yellow kilt (spun, woven, and deep-pleated using wool from his own estate flock of Cheviots). His reputation for parties, for fancy cocktails—with essences of historic berries grown on his estate and distilled in his ancient barns by ageing tenants using old family formulae that are not written down—is legendary.

In reality Jock is sitting on the throne with his trousers concertinaed around his bony, sockless, hairless ankles.

In his head he is climbing dizzy heights of commerce, sailing up through storeys of glass and gleaming steel to his walnut-lined office in the heavens where he reclines on burgundy leather and makes decisions that will affect many, including the tenants on his highland estate and the success or otherwise of his flocks, his berries, and his ability to write stuff down.

In reality Jock trips up his threadbare (of mixed brown hues) stair carpet (with missing brass stair rods) to his back bedroom in search of fresh underpants. He would dearly like to wear the tartan pair his Auntie Vera gave him for his birthday ten years ago. But alas alack they are no more. Neither is Auntie Vera.

In his head he is being answered with, 'Aye mah Laird,' to his order of 'NO LUMPY CUSTARD AGAIN, RANALD,' as he seats himself at the head of the gleaming refectory table in his grand dining hall.

In reality Jock wonders if there is any left-over black pudding he can have for breakfast, or will last night's curling pizza have to do?

In his head he is overlooking the minutiae of life, and seeking the big picture, the global scene, so to speak, opening his strong arms wide from the pinnacle of his life to embrace all.

In reality Jock looks up at sky, watching for a sign, just a tiny sign, that's all he asks, some indication that Monica is coming back to save him. To save him from himself. To save him from going to the Supersave for bacon (because Monica always brings home the bacon).

In his head he sees his princess floating down on a white stallion, he knows it is a stallion because of its well-endowed appendage. He orders his minions to bring out the orange windsocks (that have become quite twisted en route), so that his princess (in her diaphanous pink and violet attire) can land safely on the strong muscled stallion.

In reality Jock stands at the bus stop ready to wave down the number 14 bus. He plans to take a wander down the High Road to The Duke's Head where they serve the best bitter and where he might bump into someone, anyone, not necessarily Monica, but at least someone who he can be real with.

He knows now he probably shouldn't have worn his dress kilt; the plaid is quite loud, and sans underpants and that breeze, well…

He should have listened to his head.

20. It Wasn't About Bernard

You said, 'Yes,' and because you'd been brought up to be polite, you added, 'please,' when he invited you to his house. His name was Bernard. He was in your class at school, and he wore grey woollen short trousers and long socks that turned over at the top. Peeking out from one sock's turn-over was a dark green upside down 'V' ribbon.

He was six. So were you. 'Where's your Mammy?' you said.

'Work,' he replied, grinning, wielding a large kitchen knife. Hauling, under his other arm, an enormous crusty loaf to the table.

You have to admit, on looking back, that he was fairly slick with the knife as it glinted with the sun coming through his mother's kitchen window that afternoon after school. Bernard waved the knife like the swashbucklers our teacher had shown us in a picture of the Three Musketeers. The flashing blade made shiny patterns dance on the wall and ceiling like the flower fairies in your favourite story book. You both laughed. Bernard had a nice laugh, a little gruff maybe, but you liked it; it was very boy-like.

All the time you watched the dancing fairies, you knew you were really supposed to go straight home. Down Woodthorpe Road, and stop when you got to Shelthorpe Road, where your Mammy would be waiting (by the bright red pillar box with the wide black mouth) to see you across. First you'd touch index fingers like a secret code, then hand-in-hand you'd both go, singing Daisy-Daisy, skipping down the garden path (after you'd had a couple of squeaking swings back and forth on the gate with your feet on the bottom rung, both hands gripping the top one, and your face held high to the sunshine with happiness).

And then there would be tinned fruit salad (with pink cherries and bits of pear) with evaporated milk, and bread and butter for tea. Mrs. Dale's Diary would just be coming on the wireless at 4 o'clock sharp.

But Bernard was already using the carving knife. He'd hacked two doorstops of soft white bread. Pushed the glass butter dish towards you along with a sparkling jar of bright golden-orange marmalade. You copied Bernard, spreading the butter and the marmalade, then folding the bread over (something Mammy had told you was very bad manners). The bulging sandwich hardly fitted into your tiny hand. You opened your mouth as wide as you could. It was your very first taste of marmalade. You sucked on the rough chops of peel, exploring the bitterness, licking the sweetness around your lips. You'd never known such joy: the dancing fairies; the soft white bread; the salty butter; the golden marmalade. And being invited to a boy's house, that was the biggest and best thing of all.

'I've got to go,' you announced with an abruptness that startled even you, your mouth still full. Your heart pummelling in your chest. The acute vision of your angry mammy pacing on the corner of Shelthorpe Road.

Running as fast as you could down Woodthorpe Road in your red Startrites gave you a stitch for the first time in your life. Mammy was indeed waiting at the end of the road. Pacing. Shouting and screaming. You were doubled over with the pain in your side. Was this your punishment?

No, you were sent straight to bed. Absolutely no swinging on the garden gate, no Daisy-Daisy, nor skipping with Mammy down the path. And no tinned fruit for tea. But it was the absence of the secret touching tips of index fingers that hurt the most.

Under the bed covers, between the tears, you peeled back the wrapping of the chewing gum Bernard had given you as he said goodbye. You hoped Mammy wouldn't find out.

*

She plucks at the blue and white plaid blanket over her knees, pulling just at the white threads. The action is getting a little more pronounced each Sunday you visit. You look away. She lifts her silken white head and looks too, through the window of her room. You see what she sees—the red pillar box. Her misty grey, once blue, eyes flicker. You turn back to each other, touch index fingers. You feel the chill from hers against your warmth. She nods. 'I wasn't really cross with you that day when you were late, when you were little,' she says, her frail voice quivering.

'I know,' your voice, too, has become a little frail over time, after all you are just twenty years behind her. You were her firstborn. The one she protected through life, not just through childhood.

No more words, but you know that, together, you remember the day, seventy years before, when you were late home from school. When her heart must have raced with worry. When her imagination probably told her unthinkable things.

Worrying about your children is something you experienced yourself when your own were little, sending them off to school, waiting for them coming home. Their tea on the table. Sizzling Welsh Rarebit. Wagon Wheels for a treat. Watching the clock. Breathing with relief as you saw them skipping down the path swinging their satchels.

And you thought you understood how she must have felt that day when you went to Bernard's house after school instead of going straight home.

It didn't seem important as the years went by, but on a rare trip out to a beachside café, just the two of you, for some reason, you told her about Bernard. About the marmalade especially, and how, with rationing at the time, it was a wonderful experience and well-worth going to bed without your tea that day, a day you'd always remember. And yes, you confessed about the chewing gum. As you told her, you could still remember the banana/pineapple smell of the forbidden stick of Juicy Fruit when you peeled back the yellow wrapper.

You walked the beach, reminiscing. Laughing. Giggling even. Talking about that simpler early life and how much things had changed. Together you looked out over the bay, shielding your eyes from the dancing reflections.

'I thought something terrible had happened to you,' she'd said. 'You heard such terrible things. You were my lovechild and I couldn't lose you too.'

Taking both your hands in hers, she'd said, 'I remember my first chewing gum, too. He gave it to me.'

She looked up at you then, her mouth trembling, 'He was your father.' There were questions in her eyes. You could see the beginning of tears.

You slowed, then stopped and both sat in the shelter of the dunes, looking out at the nimbus clouds forming on the horizon. Both knowing something more was in the air. Watching the sea grasses pick up in the salt breezes, turning their golden undersides in waves. At the water's edge the plovers darted back and forth. You waited for her to speak.

'But the war took him from us. You are all I have of him.'

21. Convent Girls

124 was spiteful. It wasn't so much what she said—more the way she said it, with her pinched mouth, like a mouse's arse (the opinion of one of the older girls.) 124's skinny words pursed out like she was talking through her teeth with her cheeks lemon-sucked in. Her narrow, almost black eyes pierced the room when she slagged us off. We reckoned her dirty linen bag had a unique stink in the cupboard under the Big Stairs. That was where we each hung our numbered linen bags with our stuff to be washed on Fridays. But 124 was not alone; knickers from twelve-year-old girls could be pungent, something akin to stale lake water, by the end of the week.

122 was Alice, an always decent girl. Plain in looks but freckles added a touch of kindness with their shapes of zoo animals crawling over her shoulders. 124 had no freckles. Her shoulders sloped sharply so her black uniform blazer hung like bats' wings. She taught me to say 'fuck' though. And for that she had a thread of admiration from me. Grateful for that, and many things, all these years later.

120 was Jilly. Her hook in the dirty linen cupboard was next to mine. Jilly was very tall with sharp pointy elbows and knees. She'd sewn all her name tape numbers herself in big red

stitches. She had no mother by all accounts. I liked having my hook next to hers. I sometimes lifted my arm up to put around her shoulders but couldn't reach. We laughed. There's a Box Brownie photo of us somewhere.

118 was me. I did my best not to get stinky underwear. It was hard though when you are sent away to school without knowing what periods are, what sanitary towels are for. It's even harder when the school is a convent.

Nuns don't have periods Jilly told me. Jilly, who told me all about why what happens happens and what our private parts and insides are for, "later when it's time to make babies," is what she said. I asked her how she knew and she just tapped her nose like a Private Eye in the movies.

I took it all with a schoolgirl nonchalance. But it was 124 who first spotted the bloody patch on the back of my blue gingham skirt. Did I not give you 124's name? Her name was Jean. We called her Mean Jean, which was kind of mean of us as we should have given her a chance really. But twelve-year-old girls can be cruel in addition to having stinky knickers. The meaner she was to us, the meaner we were in return. But mostly we just called her 124. On looking back it was our way of dehumanising her.

The others rallied round and shielded my back from view until we made it to the dorm and they kitted me out with sannie pads—and at that moment I felt like a woman, that the world would be mine but no way would my innards be available for some brute of a man to make babies. Jilly had yet to fill me in on the details of that, but she did say there was a book in the library.

We were learning all about Clive of India in books from the library—well we were not really learning—Sister Benedict droned while we all gazed vacantly through the window, across the dusty quadrangle with the single date palm in the centre, the one we used as a wicket in rounders. Our gazes turned to horror as we saw that 124 was up the palm tree. Like a monkey. "Sister, Sister," that's Alice trying to speak softly as we were ordered—but really wanting to sound the alarm.

"Sit, child," was Sister Benedict's reaction, not looking up from her lectern. Not seeing the spectacle of Mean Jean hanging upside down with no knickers. Not seeing the other nuns carrying a ladder to rescue 124. We stood in a row by the windows, seeing our own open-mouthed reflections overlaying the scene below.

I visited Jean in sickbay when they allowed me. She had scrapes up her arms and legs but striped weals too, across her buttocks, where the discipline nun had thrashed her for 'unseemly behaviour'.

"I deserved it," she told me. "I ran out of knickers and no-one would listen. My daddy is in Saudi and I have no mummy. I had to make them listen. I couldn't keep wearing the same old dirty ones. Could I?"

I was horrified. How could we have been so cruel to our fellow student. All of us away from home. No-one to tell. Our parents paying high fees for us to be thrashed for running out of knickers.

We'd all been punished at one time or another. Mostly for climbing the palm tree for a dare.

But Jean's wasn't a dare. It was a plea.

One night I told her I was punished for playing wrong notes in piano lesson. I showed her my cracked and bruised knuckles. Told her how Sister Lawrence brought down a big stick whenever I played a wrong note in Für Elise. Made to kneel on the cold stone floor, facing a Jesus-on-the-Cross picture and recite:

Dearly beloved, blah, blah, blah... ...his holy Word, and to ask, for ourselves dee-dah-dee-dah... others, those things that are necessary for blah-blah-blah our salvation. Dah-dee-dah... may prepare ourselves in heart and mind blah-blah... let us kneel in silence, and with penitent and obedient hearts confess our sins, that we may obtain forgiveness by his infinite goodness and mercy.

Over and over until my words burbled into one and my knees seized with the cold. Until Jesus, too, went all wobbly and distant. And I hated Für Elise and Sister Lawrence. Then wondered if I should confess for hating. So straightened up and began again.

"She is making me do that too," said Jean.

***

We are in the Kyrenia hills now. Far from Nicosia and the convent. We rarely talk about those days. Sometimes we hear Beethoven on the radio and promptly switch him off. We do have a fondness for local dates though.

Why Jean and I came back together thirty years later beats me. We tried to get in touch with Jilly and Alice and eventually a letter came telling us that Alice had committed suicide—with no details. That was like a thump in the guts for sure.

We saw a newspaper article about a new nunnery too. An open facility where abused women could find refuge. What amazed us is that it was the same site as our old convent. There was a photo of the Nun Manager (a new name for Mother Superior we reckoned) and blow me down, it was Jilly. Still tall. Still all angles with her pointy elbows and knees.

We've written to her and she is promising to visit—after all we are only forty miles away in our little village villa for two.

Then she sent the news that Sister Lawrence was dying. We didn't want to think ill of her, but her cruelty was hard to forget. We did get a phone call the day she died. Jean and I knelt on soft cushions on our deck looking out over Morphou Bay and, knowing the words like it was yesterday, began to pray: 'dearly beloved...'

22. Strong and Black

A grim grey building of only thirty-four storeys. It's a shock; you expected a soaring head office tower for such a so-called prestigious company. Something designed by an architect maybe—not exactly a skyscraper like The Princess Tower in Dubai, but at least something with some clout. No—this is just one giant concrete bunker.

Mindless. Colourless. Brooding.

Out front, among the tedious line up of everyday cars, there's a stand-out electric blue '58 Chevvy; unusual in the UK and no way a standard colour either. 'CEO' says the sign. You park your own vintage, staid-and-safe '89 classic red Volvo beside it, 'Visitors Parking Only' says your sign. You cringe at the missing apostrophe.

You've driven for three hours to arrive at what can only be described as a compound. The barbed wire fence is another shock. The demonstrators blocking your access hurl obscenities. But that's all they hurl.

She's a redhead, the one who gives you the finger; she looks like the leader of the demo. You feel a long-lost but familiar pull in the belly. Try not to feel guilty.

You stopped just once for a leak and to pick up coffee and a curling pink-ham sandwich, most of which you threw into the ditch half a mile further up the road. Two sticks of dark KitKat kept you going.

Your job interview is for 2 pm. You rumble. You've missed your normal lunch of peas'n'rice. You could've opened the nuts at the bottom of your briefcase—but they are for later. When this is all over.

You swallow bland saliva, now wishing you'd given this trip a swerve and stayed put. You could have had a pudding— golden sweetness fills your head.

So you pull on the last of your Marlboroughs, pop in a Polo mint to take away both the craving for food and the smell of the cig, wriggle into your smart navy blue suit jacket and step out to talk to the guy on the gate, "Hi there, I've an appointment."

"Name?"

"Napier," you say, "Andy Napier."

"You're expected, erm… Miss," he says, hanging on to the dragging jowls of his grimace, handing you a swinging ticket on a green lanyard with your name and V I S I T O R in red.

You slip it over your head and follow the neon orange forefinger of his glove to reception.

The waiting area is all glossy glaze, all light and bright shining glass and chrome. Complete contrast to the ominous grey exterior. What a fake. There's a larger-than-life look-alike Andy Warhol painting on the wall. Red. Black. White. Lips. Lots of scarlet lips. It's hard to look away. You're told to be seated on sinkable lush cream leather; for you, that goes against the grain for starters. You look down at your canvas sandals and tuck your brown feet (with their unpainted toenails) under the furniture. You already know you should have replied 'no' to the invitation for an interview. This confirms it. Decision made. You're going to get the hell out of Dodge.

Too late, your name is called.

It's a panel interview. Five grey-bristled guys in old school ties and Austin Reed pin stripes stretched across their bulging bellies. Whisky drinkers you reckon, judging by their flushed faces and tell-tale noses. They dive right in.

"Right… …er Miss… …er Andy…, we didn't expect a… well… erm… cough… a young lady…"

"Excuse me," you interrupt, "I've driven for three hours, any chance of a coffee?"

With much kerfuffle and throat clearing a call goes out, "Linda, can you please bring... well er... Miss Napier, how would you like it?"

You know that feeling—when the bile rises—and you feel it is one of those times to speak before you put your brain in gear? That. So you do. Firm and clear, "Strong and black. Please." You draw the line at adding your usual joke.

A hush, followed by much embarrassed attempts at laughter. Linda (bless her cotton socks) brings in a cup of very black bitter coffee with two little malt biscuits (the kind you get at the hair salon) in the saucer. It's one of those large French porcelain bistro cup and saucers, dark green with squared off sides and gilded rim. You're reminded, for a brief moment, of one of those TV dramas set in the eighties where coffee is called for and it appears in crockery such as this.

You've already decided you don't want the job, and fancy reception notwithstanding, you don't want to work in a concrete block surrounded by barbed wire and demonstrators. Even more, there's no way you want to work with a bunch of stuffed shirt sexist racists.

So you dunk the biscuits in the coffee before looking up and smiling the best broad white smile you can muster. "Thank you, great coffee." You feel the quality of the sculptural sensual element of the cup while deciding if you should tell them you're off.

"We are sorry James Newingham, our CEO, cannot be here to meet you." An arm is waved at an empty chair, "he is dealing with the police regarding the demonstrators."

You nod, remember the Chevvy, and wonder if the missing, mysterious Mr. Newingham could make a difference to the way you feel. You also remember the redhead demo leader and hope she's not carted off in handcuffs quite yet.

But this bunch has got you now. Sitting back in the single green leather chair with no arms before their expansive board room table, behind which they sit in their five red leather armed versions. They each have a folder before them. Open at your CV—your glowing CV—with your years of experience. With your extensive academic qualifications. Nowhere is it stated that you are a black woman.

"I see you are a sailor," says the military tie.

"Hmmm," you say, wondering what the fuck that has to do with anything.

"Lakes?"

"Lord no," you smile wider. "Oceans."

***

Do you really want this job? Penned in? Pacing floors? Dealing with idiots? Day in day out? Your favourite painting of your love, framed on your office wall?

Of course you don't. Bugger the money. To hell with the kudos. Fuck the career ladder.

"If that's everything, I must go."

They look astounded. Blustering. Red-faced. You reckon no-one has ever questioned their authority. Their control. Their say-so.

You don't shake their hands, but, "Thank you so much for your time," you say, "and a big thank you to Linda too, her coffee was great."

And with that you swing through the gleaming reception out to your trusty Volvo and, with a cheery wave to the statue-like guy on the gate, unseeing of his gesticulations in your rear-view mirror, you drive out of the barbed wire perimeter fencing and slow beside the demonstrators.

You call across to their leader, "How's it going?"

She waves the banner and megaphone. Puts her gear down and strides across to you, "Not much happening, no-one is taking any notice. You press?"

"No, sorry, but what's your beef?"

"Poor choice of word," she says with a smile. "We are animal rights people; they are experimenting on rabbits and mice. Dogs and cats too we understand."

"Huh," you say, 'best of luck with it. My guess is all they're interested in is money. If I was you, I'd hit 'em where it hurts." Your visitor's pass is still dangling around your neck. You hand it to her, "Maybe this will come in useful. I'm getting the hell out, but if you feel like…" You exchange business cards.

You think about Emma (yes that's her name) as you drive back to Bristol. You have her card on your dash. You think about stuffed shirts in their grey prison where they have small animals penned up. You think about cages and compounds and all the people in the world who are hemmed in, kept under control, through no will of their own.

And you make your decision.

Your love is not just a picture on a wall. She's the Ida Bell, an Oyster 56 ocean-going yacht. Given to you by your father when you landed a first. But instead of climbing your career ladder up some great concrete shitbox somewhere, you will take her out to sea.

The text from Emma comes in the following week. 'Arrested last week after U left, visitors pass worked like a dream, got a warning, it was worth it. Wanna meet?'

You invite her to Bristol. To the Ida Bell. You've studied Emma's background; her website was on her card. You know she is smart, and you are looking for one person to help crew.

Emma arrives with a box. "For you," she says. Over wine and pizza she says, "Are you going to open it?"

"No, you," you say, sipping the Pinot Noir. You watch her. Her strong brown fingers unknotting the string, winding with care into a ball. The wrapping paper folded and placed aside. She opens the box and lifts out a piece of machinery.

"What the…?"

"Don't you know…?"

"Should I?" You say, touching the vane, making it rotate. And then it hits you, it is an early version of one of your digital sailing aids. "It is an anemometer," you practically scream. Jumping up. But hanging on to your wine.

"I thought it would interest you," she says, with no coyness, looking at you with a directness you've rarely experienced. "I checked out your Facebook page. This has been in my family for generations."

Over the week you plan. Together. You plot— directions—circular—Doldrums—Bermuda (triangle?)— Puerto Rico—Florida…

You feed each other green almonds, you knew she too would like the fuzzy orbs, you swallow the delicate jelly of the unripe nuts in unison. You watch her tongue peek out and catch the tiny droplet on her lower lip. "Try dipping them in this," you sprinkle sea salt into the palm of your hand. She dips, you open, she puts the half almond on your tongue just like a confirmation wafer.

You lie back together on the deck, sip Red Stripe and watch the clouds travel in a westerly direction. The wind shifts. And shifts again. The clouds seem undecided. Then scrambled. Then tormented.

It is as if the two of you are caught in a vortex.

The cups of the anemometer begin to move. Whirl. Frantically. Unable to find a direction.

You and Emma watch. But do not wonder. You have never been in a happier place than the one you are in right now. She nods and reaches for your hand. "Together," she says, "Whatever happens."

The anemometer joins the conversation: South-south-west, south, south-east, east...

23. Postcards from the Edge

Girl

She slips into the car park in a silver Mustang convertible. I look twice, wondering, for a moment, if I'm seeing things. But no, it's Gloria. All alone.

She swings out her curvy legs, and stands, for a second or two, before clipping across the car park in her silver high-heeled sling-backs. Her dress shimmers, her lipstick film-star red, her long hair buttercup-yellow.

The last time I saw her she had a mahogany urchin cut and wore Doc Marten's. But it's most definitely her. I call, "Hey Glo, how're doin'?" but she trips across to the door of the bar and disappears into the dark.

I've known Gloria since we were kids, and I always know when she's got a quest just by the way she walks, even in those ankle-breakers. There's been reports of some goings on in this neck of the woods since Christmas and if Gloria is up to her normal digging, then something's up, for sure. Always a girl for solving mysteries.

I pull my hoodie over my head and follow her into the bar.

Red

She's at the end of the bar glugging back a Guinness. Never was much of a lady. And not now neither—never mind the flash car and silver shoes, never mind the scarlet talons grabbing the glass, she's still the old Glo; more boy than girl. More man than woman. I should know.

And look-ee here who she's already hooked up with—if it isn't Red Black. His name's Ed really, Ed Black, we called him Red because of his carrot top. I reckon he liked it, reminded him of Red Adair apparently—you know that guy who used to deal with oil well fires. Gave our Red a touch of macho just knowing that.

He's drinking a Crème de Menthe in a fragile conical glass—nothing macho about him now. Anyway, they have their heads together, her yellow locks, his long red ponytail. Looks like they're cooking up something.

They've gone, and I was only in the gents a minute or two. The car's gone too. Best guess she's taken him back to hers for a bit of hanky-panky.

The mind boggles.

Spain

We first met again, as adults, in Spain on one of those forgettable long drunken weekends. The sun beat down all day and that night she rubbed calamine onto my burnt skin. It would be good to say I could feel her fingertips feathering up and down my thighs—but to be honest all I could feel was the burn.

The next day I woke to an empty hotel room. Empty of all her gear and no sign of Glo.

I've never been back to Spain. I did get the odd postcard from her though saying, *we're on the coast, come on down...* then, *get a bus to Asturius, you'll love it. I'm waiting for you...* and *The Alhambra is ab fab at this time of year. Why don't you come...?*

Gloria popped into my life once in a very long while. Like a glimmer of sunshine before the next cloud blew over. Each time she was changed. Not just stuff like colour and style of hair, but the way she talked. Once with a strong Brummie accent, the next you'd think she been in California or something. Her laugh was different too. Her genuine laugh I never heard again.

She never worked, to my knowledge. I often wondered how she did it: travel the world; designer clothes; exotic cars. All the trappings of being moneyed.

And then there was the talk of a sex change.

Behind Closed Doors

Red was adopted. He'd always known. "I had a happy childhood," he always said, but I knew different. The bruises meant something. Didn't they? And he got bullied over his pretty hair all the time. It was funny to see him just now, him with his long hair, a deep copper red. He seemed proud of it. Tossed his head like a happy colt in a meadow. Like a girl.

We got close the day it rained with no let up. We'd be about nine years old. Mam sent me out in my wellies and I called on Eddie, as we knew him then. "Can Eddie come out to play please?" I asked politely at his Mam's kitchen door.

His mam said yes but to stay out of the puddles and not to get muddy.

Of course we didn't listen to that. We jumped and splashed and laughed until we nearly weed in our trousers. It was a day to remember. A happy day.

In the days that followed Eddie didn't come out to play. He didn't go to school neither. His mam said he was right poorly.

He walked with a limp for a long while after. Then his Da went off and I don't think he ever came back.

Mind Reader?

So here am I sitting on a bench outside the bank. The town has changed a bit since I was last here; pedestrianised the High Street and a few tubs with geraniums. There's a busker outside Superdrug playing some old Formby numbers— popular with the seniors who are bobbling up and down with their Roy Cropper shopping bags. I wouldn't be surprised if they don't burst into song with, 'When I'm cleaning windows... '

That's when I spot them again: Glo and Red. Sidling into M & S. Looking furtive. I leave my copy of the local free paper on the bench for the next weary shopper and make my way into Marks and Sparks. Not been in here for yonks, but I recognise the smell. Mothballs? Cardigans? Chicken sandwiches? I'd know it blindfold that's for sure.

They're in the men's underwear department. Holding up fancy orange ones with purple stripes. Really? Does Red need new boxers? Or maybe, yes that's it, maybe they're for Glo.

"I know what you're thinking," she yells in my left ear.

I've no idea how she got from there to here—but she did.

"It's so rude," she screams with the entire floor looking on. Then she storms off with Red on one one arm and the telltale bag on her other.

Not my Game

Three more days of this heat and I think I may go back to Scotland. I can see it now, the wide open spaces of North Uist. The cool breezes coming off the Atlantic. The total lack of humans. The space to think.

But then there's my dilemma isn't there? The fact that Glo and Red appear to have a secret. A pact. I feel that I've been cut out. They have each other and I have no-one. Not that I've ever needed anyone; my 'flying solo 'motto has always suited in the past.

Then Glo texted, *Brighton is brilliant why don't you...?* Talk about deja vu. Just like when we were in Spain. And what a let down that all turned out to be. I remember her tiny hands rubbing calamine into my back. How the towel slipped and she carried right on down to my legs. And how I thought I loved her.

So, what's going on now Glo? I want to ask. But I'm scared of the answer. Is she angling for a threesome? If so, I'm not playing that game. Red's just not my type.

Greener pastures

I've not replied to Glo's repetitive texts for me to hop on the train and hook up with her (them?) in Brighton. There's more going on right now and Glo and Red can play silly knickers on Brighton Pier to their hearts 'content for all I care.

Truth is I think I've found my mother. I'm not sure if this is what I want, but after all these programmes on the telly about long lost families etc., I kind of got thinking.

I was fifteen the day she didn't come home. School was going well, I was considering my options: arts v. sciences, and sitting on the wall talking to a dark-haired girl called Carole, wondering what we would have for tea and hoping against hope that bacon would be part of it (I was going through my 'I-heart-bacon phase'). It was a day that you remember for many reasons.

The sunshine, the girl's smile, the mouthwatering anticipation of bacon, when it all fell apart. I swung down the garden path. Da was sitting on the step waiting.

"She's gone, Jim, left us," he managed to say before sobbing into his big raw hands.

Our lives changed at that moment. There was lots of bacon, one of the few things Da and I could do. But we lived with the same rooms, never changed a thing. I know now, looking back, that Mam must have done loads of things we never noticed. Washed the curtains from time to time just one example—I remember they were once bright orange, but after a few months became more brown, even grey.

And that was the home I left behind when I trotted off to Uni to study arts and languages. To greener pastures supposedly. There were still loads of bacon. And brown curtains. I dropped out after three months.

I didn't go home. I think now it's time.

Hero?

There's been, to coin a phrase, much water under the bridge. I need to put all that behind me and find the truth.

My mother replied to my letter. I was shocked, in a way. I hadn't expected her to reply really. I always thought she didn't want to be found. The letter is quite clear:

My dear wee Jimmy,

My boy I've missed you always and hope you'll understand over time why I had to leave.

I can't put too much in a letter, so why don't we meet? I can get to Glasgow if you can.

With much love, Mam.

And that was it. Or was it? I'd planned to go to Scotland to cool off but postponed that idea as I'm pretty skint. So I can't get to Glasgow—not right now anyway so I reply hoping there's somewhere closer—no, no not Brighton, don't be daft, I'm thinking Midlands. Leicester maybe.

The reply came immediately telling me she could be in a little village called Woodhouse Eaves staying at The Olde Bulls Head two weeks next Tuesday.

I hitched. It's not hard, M1 most of the way, and then I picked up a ride to Loughborough. There's a public footpath from Loughborough to Woodhouse Eaves, across the fields. It is four miles. I've done it before in another life. The footpath comes out right opposite the pub.

She is sitting in the garden drinking coffee and reading what looks like an old Penguin book—you know, the orange paperback—I always thought it was such a clever marketing idea. So recognisable.

And I know immediately it is her. She looks up, takes off her glasses and smiles. I had no idea it would be so easy. Her arms are around me as they once were when I was tiny.

"I've ordered BLTs for lunch," she says. "I hope you still love bacon."

I am speechless, but we sit and reach across the table. She smiles and says, "It's OK Jimmy, It's going to be just fine."

She tells me over lunch how she took on the undercover work. How no-one had to know. How she's been helping people. But she wouldn't say more.

I saw her through new eyes then. How she'd left us to help others.

And I don't know how to feel.

Hidden Messages

"I woke to the sound of someone throwing stones at the window." she says. "That's how it always started—they never phoned. I met them at lunchtime in the middle of the park, you know where there was once a statue of Enid Blyton."

As she talks, the old Hebridean accent starts to show. I find some comfort in that. I nod. Then shake my head because

I realise I don't know what happened to the statue. Wasn't even aware it was also gone.

"And I never came home."

It's an obvious statement. I know, as much as anyone, that she never came home, that she just disappeared—pouff! And Da and I had to get on with things.

"Did Da know?" I say.

She spreads her hands wide as if she is still throwing gravel. As if that's the explanation. "I did keep an eye on you both though."

It hit like a thump in the guts. She could see us but we couldn't see her. Un. Be. Liev. Able.

"I will go back," she says.

"Home?" I say.

"No, not home. Sorry."

And that was it. I stayed the night at The Olde Bulls Head. The next morning at breakfast there was no sign of her. "She checked out early," I was told.

So I did the same.

Beauty and the Beast

I don't know which is Beauty and which is the Beast. My old girl Gloria, or my old mate Red Black. Glo's hair is like straw now and the shadows beneath her eyes detract from what was once a face so alive, so animated, so full of life. She seems completely lived out.

Whereas Red, little Eddie as he once was, is upbeat. His laugh is musical, his bright blue eyes filled with joy. She obviously brought a new quality out in him in Brighton. Just as well I didn't make up the threesome (if that's what it was).

We're meeting in The Three Jays. There's a small back room with just one table, no jukebox, no slot machines. It's quiet. This meeting place was my suggestion and I reckon it's a good one.

"We're off to Spain," says Red.

I feel a lurch in the pit of my belly. The thought of the two of them together. The thought of Spain. I dare not ask whereabouts in Spain. I don't want to know.

"Come with us," says Glo. Her face suddenly a glimmer of the old Glo. A look of hope. A question in her eyes.

"Sorry to disappoint," I say. "I'm off to Scotland. Probably for good."

Back to Scotland

It's been a long day of travelling. Glad to receive the tickets from my mother—that helped enormously—she must be paid well at whatever this secret job of hers is.

***

There are times when you stand on a land and know that it is just the right place for you to be. I'm getting the ferry from Uig later but now I stand and bow my head to Duntulm. It sits proudly, if a little war torn in the distance. But the castle speaks to me of a time in my past of which I have no recollection.

119

The sheep graze in the field beneath as if totally unaware of what might have happened centuries ago on that self-same field. I swallow hard. The others seem so far away now, in a different world altogether. I don't need them in my life. I have to acknowledge that knowing both of them made me—well partly anyway—the man I am today. And I wouldn't change that.

It's almost 2 pm now and the ferry leaves shortly. In a couple of hours I'll be there. To the island I should always have called home, but never dared.

From the rails of the MV Hebridean I will watch Skye disappear. And wait not too patiently for Lochmaddy to appear on the horizon. I will hear the chunter of familiar excited tongues as we pull into the jetty.

I will not scour the small crowd of waiting families and friends for my mother. I know she will not be there.

24. Emergence

There was once a song: *...everybody loves Somebody sometime...* and it caught Jennifer by the throat each time she heard it. 'But Nobody loves me...' was her wail. 'Why has love deserted me?'

'Am I just a Nobody? A Nobody just waiting for a Somebody?' They told her at school that if she wanted to make something of herself, be Somebody. Then she'd have to buck up; open up; speak up. Get up off her lardy backside.

But all this 'up' stuff was way too high for Jennifer. Being a Nobody had its comforts; she could crawl away after school, and later—after work. Slouching home in her frumpy grey skirt and black lace up shoes. Back to her dingy flat which she thought of as her hole in the ground. The place where she microwaved her bowl of macaroni cheese and ate ice cream straight from the container. Where she picked her nose and broke wind through all the TV soaps because Nobody was watching.

In 1982 she woke to the fact that a Nobody could love a Nobody too. Maybe, just maybe there was another Nobody out there waiting to be loved. This after she heard the new song *Nobody* on the radio: *...but I can love you like Nobody can, even better...*

That's all it took. She booked herself a haircut and a facial. She ate salads and drank water for a month. She bought herself a pair of red stilettos.

She succumbed to buying four yards of purple silk and after work made a dance dress, edging it with sequins. The following Saturday evening she emerged: Jenny.

The dancehall was swinging. But all eyes swerved to take in the new girl on the block as Jenny stepped through the double doors, her dark brown hair shining in the disco lights.

She really felt like Somebody. But she knew what a Nobody could feel like and she spotted one, a wallflower hiding away behind a potted palm. She walked over and tapped the Nobody's shoulder. "Hello," she said, my name is Jenny, would you like to dance?"

The Nobody looked up into Jenny's deep brown eyes and said, "Thank you so much, I never thought Somebody would notice me here, my name is Joan and I'd love to dance."

25. Trip of a Lifetime

"Is that really what you've done?" she says. Too tired for tears. Too exhausted to be angry with him. "I thought we always said we would never..."

Ginger slumps into her old armchair. Still in her red and white tabard uniform from the diner. Her legs ache. Her back aches. And now a dull nagging ache that Mel has gone against their pledge, the one they have upheld all their married life: never to borrow.

He looks up at his wife with the sideways sheepish glance she has come to know; a sign that he has gone behind her back. "Sweetie, my Sugar-pie, I didn't mean to. I honestly had no intention of borrowing the money. But I just couldn't help myself," he says. "There was the giant poster in the loan company's window, with the Empire State Building, saying, 'you could take a trip of a lifetime' and I thought, yes we could, yes we can, and so, yes I did. And you know I'd do anything for you. If we don't go now, we never will, so yes, I borrowed the $100 we needed so we can go."

Ginger gasps. It is the longest sentence she's heard from her husband in years. Borrowing money, their big no-no. Doing it without talking it through even worse. But his sheepish look has turned to love and determination now, and she's tired. She nods in slow acceptance.

In the days that follow, excitement and anticipation start to creep in, finally working their way to her face which breaks into the big wide smile and shining blue eyes she's known for.

So Ginger and Mel are going to New York. The news is out. It is their trip of a lifetime. Her workmates at the diner give Ginger all kinds of advice:

"You have to go to Carnegie Hall."

"And Ground Zero, that's a must."

"Don't forget the Statue of Liberty."

"And the Empire State Building, just like King Kong."

Ginger listens and nods. Long ago, she decided what she would do if she ever got to New York. She and Mel saved for years for this trip and it was never quite enough. As soon as they had the right amount, the cost would soar again. They've never been outside of Albion Pennsylvania before, not even for their honeymoon over forty years ago. "It is our trip of a lifetime," they say to each other. "No-one else's. Ours."

She sends off for tickets for Wheel of Fortune. A chance for her and Mel to see the famous Rick and Trisha in the flesh would be like a dream come true. Rick with his Caribbean tan and Trisha in her long spangled cocktail dress, the wheel spinning and the contestants screaming themselves silly when they win; Ginger wants it all. When the tickets arrive in the mail, she feels like her belly is full of purple balloons, she's that excited.

Mel and Ginger go to New York for three days. They arrive on Tuesday afternoon and check into the Hotel Pennsylvania in Midtown, Manhattan. It's less than $100 a night but they choose it for more than the value deal, they guess it will be like a home away from home. Ginger doesn't intend they spend much time there, no sirree; she and Mel are going to get themselves all dressed up and go for a real New York pizza, then head right to Radio City Music Hall. She wants to line up early and watch all the comings and goings.

Mel puts on his new navy blue shirt Ginger found for him at the Goodwill and wets his comb at the basin in the corner of the room. The comb leaves furrows of pink as his scalp shows through his sparse grey hair. He smiles at his reflection; it is the smile of a man who, at long last, can give the woman he loves, something she deserves.

For the theatre Ginger wears a sunshine yellow polyester blouse with loose flowing white pants. She ordered them from the Sears Roebuck catalogue and paid them off over six months. The size eighteen turned out to be too snug, so she phoned the nice girl who told her how to send them back in the original packaging.

"What d'ya think?" she said to Mel when the size twenty-somethings finally arrived. She held them up against her and sashayed around the kitchen. "Do you think Rick will spot me in this yellow, on the fifth row? Won't we look swell, you in your leather jacket and your cowboy boots, and me in this?"

The night starts out just as she imagined. Ushers keep the audience amused before the show starts. They are told to clap when the green lights flash, and keep quiet when the red light is on, especially when the contestants are answering. "Also," they are told, "we are being broadcast right across North America."

"Just think Mel," says Ginger, "they could even see us on TV back home."

"Hush, Sweetie," says Mel, "they are making an announcement. It's you. They are asking for you. You're the red-headed lady in yellow on the fifth row? Aren't you?"

Ginger looks behind her, and around her, then in front, where the ushers are beckoning for her to go forward. "Me?" she points to her generous yellow-enveloped bosom.

"Yes, you Honey, the lady in the sunny yellow, please come forward and bring your handsome man with you."

Mel and Ginger make their way along the row, saying, "Sorry, pardon me," until they reach the aisle.

"One of our contestants is sick and dropped out," she is told. "You have been chosen as our replacement." Ginger can't believe her ears. Her face begins to flush the colour of their front door back home.

Mel nods to her and whispers, "Your dreams really are coming true, I love you, don't be scared Sweetie, I'll be waiting."

Ginger is shepherded backstage to hair and makeup and within minutes joins Rick and Trisha and the other contestants on stage. Sound checks prove that Ginger's voice is 'hell yes' strong enough, and the show gets underway.

The wheel spins. Ginger has seen the show so many times, the clues are obvious. She spits them out almost before the wheel stops. And then, quick as a chipmunk scurrying under the woodpile, she's won $43,000 and is in the bonus round.

"And who do you have with you?" says the tanned Rick.

"My wonderful, loving husband, Mel," says Ginger, who's witnessed the scene every night on the TV back home, she can say the words in her sleep.

The bonus wheel is spinning, it lands on W. She reaches out her plump finger and thumb and, without a tremble, plucks up the card. Rick takes her warm hand in his cool one and together they look at the board as the clues are filled. Of course Ginger knows the answer. "Boiled cabbage," she says, without hesitation.

Rick opens the card. Ginger all but faints when he announces that she has won another $100,000. Before she knows it, she is in Mel's arms.

"I had no idea you were so clever," he whispers.

"I had no idea either," says Ginger. "Is this for real?"

"I reckon so, Sweetie," says Mel. "I guess all our worries are over now. And I can pay back the $100 I borrowed."

They take a yellow cab back to the Hotel Pennsylvania in Manhattan. They sit on the edge of the pink slippery bedspread and hold on tight to each other. They promise that this will not change a thing; that they won't be rash; this is the most unexpected windfall they could ever have hoped for, and they will be putting most of it away for a rainy day.

Before they go home they will shop in New York, after all, this is their trip of a lifetime. They will go to 5th Avenue and buy Mel a soft green doeskin shirt from L.L. Bean, a pair of handmade Laredo cowboy boots and one of those fancy watches that can be worn underwater. Ginger will invest in a digital camera from the Nikon store and a fuchsia silk blouse from Bloomingdales. They will 'do' New York and take in the sights: The Statue of Liberty; Ground Zero; The Carnegie Hall, and they'll go as high as they can up the Empire State Building. Lunch on their last day will be at the Plaza Hotel where they'll watch a different world pass before them.

Ginger will be amazed that the cute little piece of plastic that goes into the Nikon camera will hold hundreds of pictures. She will snap and snap with abandon, just like the salesman showed her, so that when they get back home she can pop it into a new flatscreen TV. Their friends and family and workmates will be invited to a 'Big Apple' party where they'll be shown Mel's and Ginger's pictures.

But the best picture of all will sit, in a gold-plated frame, on the mantle shelf. It is the official photo of Ginger and Mel standing with a tanned Rick and pretty, sequin-gowned Trisha on the stage at the Radio City Music Hall.

26. More so

You hated geometry at school. Calculus, more so.

You loved your gold braided, forest green blazer with the inside pocket. The hunky maths teacher, more so.

His garlic breath was unexpected as he closed in to guide you through complex calculations. His hairy-backed hand closing over your slender pale one didn't give you the buzz you'd anticipated. How he managed to slip the note into your inside pocket will always be a mystery. Why you didn't shiver as his hand brushed your left breast, more so.

Shoeboxes full of love notes, great for your memoirs. But fiction, more so.

27. Blue white gold

One.

Gavin opens his eyes but doesn't see the blueness of the sky, doesn't leap from his bed to face the day, instead he rolls over and thinks about his life, a life he never wanted, even as a child he would wail, 'I didn't ask to be born,' as most children did and then got on with things and that's what he's telling himself now, as he has done every morning as long as he can remember, 'I've just got to get on with things, but what things,' he wonders, 'should I wash and wax the car? After all it is Sunday,' but the car hasn't been used for weeks now, just can't be bothered to look for the keys and he reckons Alice must've hidden them somewhere as she probably knows what he'd do if he could drive to the edge of the cliff at full speed and forget all about brakes, and say to himself while he was doing it, 'that'll teach them all to be nonchalant about life, about my life in particular,' but he can't find them—that's his keys and his wife—so he tiptoes downstairs in his bare feet, well bare everything really, carefree for the first time in his life, and makes himself a cup of tea and as he tastes that first cup of the day he tells himself, 'that's good, it ain't all bad then.'

Two.

Zola opens her eyes but doesn't see the blueness of the Aegean, doesn't see the idyllic view that was there when she dozed off in the golden sunshine an hour earlier, when she drifted with the soporific lulling of the gentle waves lapping ashore from the turquoise waters of the cove, doesn't see because of the long shadow cast over her, a shadow of someone she feared that she'd come all this way to avoid, the someone who'd given her just cause to hoppit to the Greek Island on a cut-price last minute package deal from Gatwick to Symi where goats cling to hillsides, chewing at wild garlic among golden windowless homes that are a haunting reminder of WWII when the island was occupied and from which local people were changed forever but because of their stalwart outlook made a remarkable recovery and who had freely given Zola solace and shelter from the oppression of her tormenter, 'Found you,' he says and she recognises the voice of Aristotle and smiles, 'your coffee and baclava are ready,' he tells her as she sits, looks out at the deep blueness of the far horizon realising there is not a sign of Roger at all.

Three.

Ian opens his eyes but doesn't see the multi-colours of the heavy linen curtains (with William Morris bluer than blue peacocks) draped at the windows of his mother's bedroom, neither does he know how he finished up, completely naked, in the four poster bed that he, apparently, was born in, it seems to him that to be in his birthday suit in his mum's bed is probably quite appropriate but then he wonders who in the hell took his clothes off and btw where the hell are they—a question for which there are no answers as there is no-one else

in the room, and no-one is answering his calls of, 'helloooo…
is there anyone out there…' so he hops across the glorious rich
red of the threadbare (yes it is in places) Persian rug to the
window to fling it wide and call out only to find that the
windows have all been bolted shut with one of those modern-
day window keys and so Ian hops back to the bed, which is
sumptuous btw and snuggles under the modern-day duvet,
gently drifting into one of those afternoon slumbers that are
not like another sleep until a light tap on the door, which
wasn't locked btw, and in steps a waiter (called Myles) with a
silver tray of tea and biscuits, singing, 'Wakey wakey' in true
Billy Cotton style, at which Ian sits up, accepts the tea and is
not one bit embarrassed about his naked state or the fact that
he is dunking his digestives in the Earl Grey.

Four.

Roger opens his eyes but doesn't see a thing, he stumbles
from his bed in the attic and glimpses how the world has
turned white in the night—70 cms according to the faint (or
is it fake?) news he hears whispering its way from below to his
distant attic bed, a toasted crumpet and a cup of rosy-lee
would be just perfect is his one thought as he pulls on the thick
white fisherman socks she knitted for him when she loved him
and when he loved her—the only things he has left to remind
him of that other life when he and Zola curled up in their big
bed together like fiddlehead ferns in the spring ready to uncoil
and face a day of joy and wonderful happenings—but it was
his fault he supposes that she uncoiled one day and walked out
the door and never came back—and his fault that he has spent
every uncoiled waking hour trying to find her—to track her

down—to 'talk it through' like the internet has told him to do—but he guesses this is a lost cause now and that if she is out in this storm with the gales and the ice and snow there is little chance she'd be found alive anyway, but is that the aroma of toasting crumpets he asks himself, pulling on a red tartan dressing gown that once belonged to some other poor outcast bugger and pads his way in the thick off-white socks down to the roomy pink and white kitchen with the giant table sporting blue and white striped plates on its sparkling white table cloth and Rick says 'sit down old buddy, I've made your favourite' and together they look out at the whiteness of the world both thinking it is washing them clean all the worries of the past and clink their big blue enamel mugs with a 'cheers buddy' while letting melted butter from the piping hot crumpets trickle down their unshaven chins.

Five.

Aristotle opens his eyes and doesn't see his wonderful country's blue and white flag or the gold dome of Ayios Andreas but that's because the sun is so bright all he sees are black dots which means he completely misses the crocodile of weary tourists heading to his bar, and he should know better for it is 4 o'clock, the time the tour bus gets in from Rhodos, he has no idea what the stalker Roger looks like even though Zola has described him as a gorilla with blue eyes and he doesn't know what that's supposed to mean either but he knows Zola needs protection and while he has been napping under the date palm he has not been super-attentive as he promised himself (and her), however, as he rouses, pulls his baggy shorts up over his belly and tightens his belt he feels positive about his life and can't see how anyone can put a spanner in his works, (that's a saying that Zola has taught him), and makes his way to his beachside bar before the tourists find it and where he makes Zola's coffee in a copper briki, pours its dark pungency into a tiny white cup, pours iced water into a tall glass and then watches the golden glints of the Metaxa as he pours it into a brandy glass, hears the crispy chunk as it hits the ice cubes and with a squirt of underarm deodorant in all the appropriate places, bristles his moustache, fixes his smile and makes his way, with the tray, to the cove and Zola—he had no premonition that she would not be there—he had no forethought that she wouldn't stick to her routine, to their plan and without spilling a drop of coffee, water or brandy he hightails it back to his bar to find her sitting on one of his barstools in a white jump-suit with white slingback sandals smoking a cigarette in a gold cigarette holder, 'Thought I'd surprise you this time,' she says and as Aristotle's heart stops thumping, he slides the tray before her then smiles at the plethora of tourists also waiting and says, 'Yes please, you like drink?'

Six.

Alice opens her eyes but sees none of the golden glory she saw in her mind's eye in those limbo moments before fully waking. All she sees now is stuff that needs fixing. Why she bought a chateau in France she has no idea other than she'd watched one episode of a TV show where everything looked more glamorous than she could have hoped. And the price— how could she resist? But how can she fix the monstrosity (because that's how she sees it now)? She stretches her long slim brown legs, slips her painted toes into pink fluffy mules, wraps her turquoise silk robe (the one with the embroidered scarlet dragon on the back) around her slender shoulders and makes her way down the grand staircase to the over-rated antique kitchen with its rusty taps and cobwebby windows.

She longs for tea. Even coffee would suffice now, but there is no water. A plumber is due at 8 and she wonders what timekeeping is like in this part of the world. No sooner has she had the thought when she sees him coming down the long driveway in an antique azure blue van with S. Jacques Plombier in gold scroll along the side and she takes a deep breath.

Over coffee (yes, he brought that with him in a very continental looking stainless-steel thermos) they talk of all things except plumbing. They talk of wine and music and history. His name is Sacha and he is the direct opposite of Gavin. He is dark with deep brown eyes. Before he leaves, he says in his exotic English, 'I will come back later and help you fix everything. Au revoir, I will return.'

Seven.

The young man who brought coffee
in his blue plumber's van
has a name like a girl's
and dark glossy tumbling curls.

He talks about his mother's love

for a French singer of romance
he stirs his coffee slowly
silver spoons overflow with honey.

When he left he left behind circle
stains—brown rings from coffee cups
circles linking chains in loops
along with sticky shiny silver spoons.

He did not return in the blue plumber's van
no longer brought steaming coffee
no longer called her Natasha—
the young man named Sacha.

Eight.

Natasha screws her eyes closed so she cannot see; if she
cannot see maybe this will not be real. She reaches down
between the crisp white hotel room sheets, under the crisp
whiter-than-white plump hotel duvet, becomes aware that she
hasn't a stitch on, becomes even more aware that there is
another naked body beside her—a hairy male body to boot,
and finds his hand. Her fingers explore his strong fingers until
they reach the gold wedding band. Confirming that he is a
married man. It must have been the drink; she must have been
off. her. rocker., must have been right off her head, she
reckons. Then slowly the dawn of realisation happens.
Realisation that the party was, in fact, her party. That it was

all about her and this male person lying beside her in the white hotel room with the crisp white bedding that smells of the sea. She takes her hand away from his and feels for her own left hand—there it is: the gold band on her finger that symbolises the step she must have taken before she got drunk. She wonders what his name might be and if she likes him—loves him even. Natasha opens her eyes to find the room is very blue—not the white of her mind (although the bedclothes are bright white still) and her bed fellow is the love of her life who she married just yesterday and they are on a Greek island for their honeymoon. And she says to herself, 'What the fuck have I done?'

Nine.

Gavin has an eye-opener and makes up his mind. This will be his blue period. And for that he must go to Montmartre. That's in France, right? His preparation includes a visit to the art shop where he invests in canvasses and paints, brushes and charcoal. He knows Alice would say, 'you can buy all that stuff when you get there you know,' but right now Alice is not in his head and for once he needs to do his own thing. And this will be it. He will be rich and famous with art exhibitions in London, Paris, New York and Madrid. He can see it now, see the posters, see the adverts: Gavin Wardrop's Blue Period with every and all the shades of blue like the surface of the sea blended with something akin to those old water-marked marbled 'inside the covers' of antique books. The posters will make people's mouths water. And with that he decides that Montmartre and the Left Bank of the Seine will not be blue enough so he heads straight from the art shop to the travel agent's to buy a ticket to a Greek Island on Friday.

On his way home he stops and sits outside a coffee shop in the precinct. He sips and thinks about what he has done and what he will do. And none of this involves Alice.

Ten.

In the history of art, only three colours were of real importance: blue and white and gold, spouts the narrator of the documentary. Natasha drowses through the programme but mutters, 'Gold is not a colour, idiot,' to the TV. She turns, in the ornate four-poster in one of the many bedrooms at her chateau and watches the gentle soul snoozing beside her, runs her fingers through his curls. She's pleased she changed her name from Alice. After all, it would never have really couple-worked with Sacha.

Zola watches the same programme in her hotel room on her blue paradise island, she sips her brandy and whispers to the TV, 'If you've never been here you don't know blue, idiot.' She phones down to Aristotle at the bar and asks him if he'd like to bring the brandy bottle and join her.

Roger and Rick are curled up together on the lumpy but comfy chintzy sofa, a fire gently flickering in the cottage grate. They look at each other and roll their eyes, then down at their matching creamy-white, miniature poodles, Crumpets and Buttered, who jump up and snuggle in beside them.

Ian and Myles have the TV playing while they decorate Ian's mother's house. They've decided red is the colour trend this year and totally ignore the programme purporting blue white and gold.

And what of Gavin? Why, he has made it BIG in the world of creativity and is narrating a TV programme about how the three colours, blue, white and gold have played such a major part in art history.

28. The Blackout

She has a fine thread of silken white hair tickling her pale forehead. She puffs through pursed dry lips, the hair lifts but falls back. I lean across and smooth away the annoyance. Ma smiles then, and mouths, "Thank you." The scar on the paper-thin skin of her forehead looks angrier now than it did when I first asked her, years ago.

She told me about it one afternoon when I was sixteen. I still don't know if it was the truth. Or whether she was telling porkies as she often did in those days. For fun. For a joke. To make her past more exciting. To entertain us kids.

"I bumped into a man in the blackout," she said. "Coming home from a dance. You've no idea what it was like. You couldn't see a thing. It wasn't called the blackout for nothing, you know. But I knew my way like the back of my hand. It'd been a lovely dance with a great RAF band. So I was still humming Chattanooga Choo Choo, feeling my way up Beacon Avenue, then wham."

I remember the first time she told me. I could see it; I know Beacon Avenue, not quite like the back of my hand, but

I did wonder what it must have been like during the war. Her war. With no street lights, no golden glows from living room windows. Finding your way by touch, past splintery front fences and gates, crossing the black-as-fresh-liquorice side roads on wet moonless nights, listening for a bicycle or one of those rarities, a vehicle. With no lights.

Taking chances. Attempting to carry on as normal. In the dark.

But what of the man she said she'd bumped into? Ma's not tall, so he must have been very short with something sharp in his top pocket to cause that scar. I often wondered about him too. Was he hurt? Did Ma take him home with her to get cleaned up?

The scar across her forehead is over three inches. There are times when it reddens and I wonder if she feels it and revisits that night. There must have been blood. And what did her father, my Grandpa, say as she stumbled through the back kitchen door after eleven? Blood trickling across her face and dripping its way through the midnight blue dance dress she'd made herself. There's a photograph of her in that dress. Eyes shining. Fair hair cascading over her shoulders. Her smile filled with anticipation. Holding someone's hand as if to begin a tango. The dress had swirls of sequins. She cut it up years later, making doll's clothes for my Caroline. It was silk.

I'd asked her a few questions over the years, but she'd just smiled saying, "It was so long ago, Dear, I can't really remember." And then, "You mustn't forget, there was a war on." As if that explained everything.

It didn't explain everything of course. Not the other scars. Those my siblings hadn't seen. I knew about those. I'd heard them happen. The stifled screams in the night. The thuds of wood on flesh. Of fist on abdomen. She'd hidden them well. But there were times I could see them in her eyes when she sat looking through the window not seeing what was going on beyond.

She has other scars. There's one that stretches the length of her forearm. Reminding me of better times.

It was a beautiful day on the edges of Chisbury Woods. Ripe blackberries dripped in abundance from the bramble hedges. We, that's Ma, the three little ones, and me, for some reason wearing my new primrose yellow cotton dress, set off brambling. We took buckets and baskets. And a couple of walking sticks, those with a crooked handle so we could hook the berry canes closer for easier picking.

I'd seen the best clumps of all, deep in the hedgerow, and was about to reach for them when Ma said, "No Lizzie, let me," I guess she didn't want blackberry juices to stain my new dress. Without one of the walking sticks she stretched in and plucked the ready-to-eat berries. But her arm ripped on

143

bramble thorns, leaving a row of scarlet stitches from wrist to elbow. We mopped her up with our hankies. She smiled and said, "It's nothing, a mere scratch. Here, let's eat these on the way home, we'll have too many for pies."

A day I'll not forget in a hurry. And I don't think she will either. I've watched her rub that scar left by the aggressive blackberry cane, and smile, over the years. Maybe we both can still taste those summer-sweet blackberry juices and feel the afternoon August sun on our backs.

We're all old now and cherish those few happier days. I'm not sure if the others stop to wonder if things could have been different. Like I do.

Mostly, though, I wonder who he was, the man in the blackout. Was he real? Did he remain in her life? Somewhere. Somehow.

I smooth her forehead and stroke the back of her hand, the one I've always known, like the back of my own.

29. Girl in a Green Dress

She wears a pale green dress in watered silk for Lysander's funeral. Her mother, being a potter, would have called it celadon, her grandmother, being a bit of a lush, would have classed it chartreuse. But to Mae it is her new green dress with a handkerchief hem and a cross-over (minimizer) bodice. Lysander picked it out with her the day they decided to get wed.

But now there will be no wedding.

If only she hadn't been deep in trying to fiddle the taxes when he first yelled for help. If she hadn't plugged her iPod firmly into her ears to get the very best from Tom Petty's Highway Companion in full throttle, she might have heard his screams. And, as keeps battering through her mind like a woodpecker in an apple tree, if she'd been out there helping him with his bees none of this would have happened.

The autopsy showed a sting on Lysander's neck. It perplexed the lab for some time until their young intern announced, "I reckon it was one of those Carpenter bees. They are quite rare, and I have no idea why it would be among the regular honeybees." She flushed slightly; it was her first breakthrough in demonstrating her expertise. "If only someone could have got to it within the first twenty minutes with vinegar, it might have stopped the poison entering the blood stream," she added with a new found confidence.

No one mentioned the vinegar to Mae, she would have disputed it anyway with: "bicarb for bees, vinegar for wasps."

Mae now has Lysander's death certificate. *Cause of Death: Asphyxia due to a Carpenter Bee sting.* The certificate is tucked squarely in the bottom of her canvas tote bag as she makes her way to the red brick Methodist chapel.

The rain started earlier in the day and Mae had no choice but to pull on her sun-shiny yellow Doc Martens. They were another of Lysander's suggestions. "You need something better than those old wellies of yours, Girlie," he said last month in Market Street when they were shopping for rhubarb, "look at these, just the job, and they've got purple spots - right up your alley."

And so he bought them for her, and while they don't really go with celadon (or chartreuse) green silk, they match Mae's conflicting feelings this damp funereal morning.

Strains of A Whiter Shade of Pale float down the aisle as she clomps her way to the front pew. Mae is Lysander's only mourner. She smiles up at Clive, the organist, and nods. The funeral is brief and, as Lysander is trundled back down the aisle and out to the cemetery for burial, Clive begins to belt out Mungo Jerry's "In the Summertime," and Mae knows, in that instant, that Clive will be her saviour.

30. Loved to Death

'Call him Benny," they said, 'Benny the Bunny."

I wrinkled my nose making my freckles run into each other and chose, instead, to name him Donald. At the time I loved to listen to Donald Piers playing the piano on the wireless on Friday nights; the only night I was allowed to stay up until eight o'clock. I liked his piano playing. Pretty songs with no words. Bobbitting up and down. Like tiny footsteps with silver bells tiptoeing on the stairs.

I was six when they gave me Donald. He was the colour of pepper and salt mixed together. I know that because I sprinkled two heaps from Nanny's salt and pepper pots, then stirred them together on her fresh scrubbed kitchen table until the patterns I made looked just like Donald. I got a lot of tutt-tutting and then a smack bottom for being wasteful and making a mess.

His eyes were blue. The same as Grandpa's hydrangeas. The ones he put his old razor blades under to make them change colour. "As good as iron filings," he told me when I asked why.

I asked "why" a lot in those days. And I got answers. Mostly about gardening and plants, and bright coloured newts in the well. I remember the answers better now than I did all those years back. And that's why the memories of what happened to Donald are clearer now too.

1948 was a hot summer. It followed the coldest winter. Everyone was so busy as if they were frightened the weather would turn on them and ruin everything. The black currants had to be picked and made into jam. The sweet peas gathered into bunches, tied with raffia and sold from the front gate. The tomatoes needed their extra leaves nipping so all the goodness would go to make them juicier. And everything always needed watering.

July drifted into August and Donald was my constant companion. My only other friend, Kathleen, was sent away to ballet school in London. Donald's nose twitched when I told him all about Kathleen, on her pale pink pointed satin shoes, in the big city with no grass.

Once the weather got hot, I had to stop him snuggling under my fair isle jumper. My mammy knitted the jumper in the colour of porridge with strands of blue and red wool. It had a pretty pattern on the outside, but inside the colours wound and bound around each other. Donald fitted perfectly in the hollow just beneath my rib cage, tickling my tummy. I felt the warmth of his body against my bare skin. The tiny beat of his heart tapped its rhythm with mine. That is what Donald liked best. He closed his eyes, slowly, when he was happy.

On Saturday afternoons Grandpa took me to cricket matches. I wore my white organza dress with the sticking-out skirt and my red blazer with brass buttons. Lying on my back looking at the clouds, listening to the cricketers and the bees, grubbing around on the cricket field, is what I remember from those summer Saturday afternoons. Then it was home to a 'fish and fruit' tea of poached smoked haddock and tinned peaches with Carnation.

Donald was waiting for me. Always. I blew softly into his fur so that I could see his pale soft grey undercoat; he knew that would be the first thing we'd do because he turned around so that I blew against the grain of his coat. Then I twiddled my fingers deep into his fur before turning him towards me and burying my face into his, breathing in his smell of warm wet tea. I gave him the outside lettuce and cabbage leaves that Nanny put out for him and settled him in his own bed for the night, with a cuddle and nose kisses before I was lifted onto the kitchen draining board to have the grime scrubbed from my hands and knees before bed.

The heatwave in the middle of August saw the entire household going for afternoon naps, leaving me to my own devices. Well, me and Donald really. They were drowsy afternoons, so I made myself a little spot behind the garden shed between the hydrangeas. A place where no-one would find us. And that is where Donald and I took our afternoon naps too. Snuggled up close together.

We were asleep when they found us some time after five o'clock. They'd been calling for ages. I'm surprised I didn't hear them, because Mrs. Dale's Diary was on the wireless at four and I heard the opening music coming through the window. They even asked the neighbours if they'd seen me. I suspected I was in for another spanking.

They prised Donald from my arms. "No, please don't take him, he's asleep and he is so cold, I want to love him warm again." I said.

"You have loved him so much, you loved him to death," they said. "He has gone to live with Jesus now."

I turned seven that year and they told me there was no Santa Claus. For Christmas I received a pair of rabbit fur gloves. The colour of pepper and salt. I put them on. Slowly. Then blew gently against the fur. And there was the soft pale grey undercoat.

31. The Sequence Dance

She left me up in the minstrel gallery overlooking the dance floor below. "You'll get your best view from here," she said before bustling back down to the dance hall.

So I am alone, looking down on a haze of expectation and an empty circle of light, when the announcement is made: *The Valentino Swing*. Two figures, hands clasped aloft, emerge into the spotlight. They are the leaders. She turns to him in a swirl of smiles and blue silk. The band strikes up a Benny Goodman number.

They dance a sequence of steps to 16 measures of music. I've been informed that each precise step is named. A chassé leads to a promenade and a feather. A cucaracha follows a fan and a shoulder-to-shoulder turn. I understand it helps to count each sequence of steps. With elegance and flair, the demonstration of the sequence is performed by the leaders. He tweaks his blue silk bowtie and she inclines her head in acknowledgement as their leading solo ends.

After a brief applause there are muffled scufflings around the edge of the dance floor as members of The Old Town Hall Sequence Dance Club rise. Some have walking frames, some have help from care workers. Many hobble to take their partners on the dance floor.

Like dusty snowflakes, gentle drifts of light from the rotating ballroom globe stir the hall alive. *The Valentino Swing* continues, the floor now filled with motion. The walking aids seem to be replaced with wings as the veteran dancers float with poise and perfection around the floor. The concentration of counting steps not visible on their radiant faces.

I half close my eyes, absorbing the shifting kaleidoscope below. It has the beauty of a giant, jewel-embellished jellyfish as it pulsates. Swelling, then changing shape in a streamlined fashion as the dancers dance the sequence. Moving in the same direction, turning in unison, flashing sequins, pointing toes in their bright satin and patent dance shoes. Tilting heads at identical angles. Bow-tied gentlemen support partners in matching manner. The floor swirls with one sweep of light and colour. Then a united pause, as damselflies would shiver over iridescent still waters before changing course.

My fingers keep time with the band and the steps of the dancers. I feel a belonging to this body of thrumming life far below. That it is me. I am the fuchsia pinks, the periwinkle blues, the violets and saffrons of the rustling dresses; they run through my veins. The flashes of sequins, and glints of gold and silver are my senses. The rhythm of music is my pulse too. I am one with the dance. Lost in the sequences.

The last strains of the Benny Goodman tune hang in the air as the band plays the final chord. The dancers too, chassé their final steps. Together. The joyous sound is replaced by murmured shuffling as care workers rush forward with comforting arms to help dancers return to their seats.

The floor below is empty except for a lone figure, her midnight blue silk dress trimmed with sequins. In her silver shoes. With her wide smile. She waves to me, beckoning me down. "Did you see us?" She says, eyes sparkling, as I arrive, breathless, at her side. "What did you think? How did we look?"

32. Chasing Rainbows

Red

"The parrot tulips this year are the most extraordinary shade of crimson," splutters Ruby with her mouth full of cream crackers, crumbs scattering like ivory dandruff down her complex, scarlet, hand-knitted (by her grandmother) sweater. Her mother doesn't knit. Doesn't watch her enormous daughter. Is not one iota interested in tulips (or cream crackers for that matter.) She wants to get away from the drudgery of caring for a thirty-year-old who is beyond lazy, who is addicted to growing expensive exotic tulips thanks to an absentee father who just throws money for the girl to fritter.

Ruby's mother, Ophelia, is unhearing of her daughter's progressive rasping and wheezing, the gasping for air. She turns up Pat Boone crooning Red Sails in the Sunset on her iPod while planning the hows and wherefores of escaping this life.

Orange

The juices of the blood orange trickle down Oscar's chin beard and get no further. He has sliced the orange into boats, and bites right in as far as the bitter pith. No-one is watching, or so he thinks, as he bares his teeth to get seriously into the task. He picks up the long bristly pointy ends of his greying facial hair between forefinger and thumb and sucks, tasting the hints of orange along with the rich yolk of his breakfast soft-boiled egg with soldiers. This is all intermingled with traces of HP sauce from last Wednesday's Cumberland sausage dinner.

He is waiting for Ophelia. She has promised faithfully she will sail away with him. 'Into the sunset', is how he described it. He has invested in a bottle of Grand Marnier so that he can make Pheelie's favourite drink as they sail down the Ouse and out into the Humber before they hit The Continent and all its mysteries.

And here she is, sheathed in a cotton lawn (vaguely diaphanous) sundress the colour of marigolds. She carries a straw bag, the same shape as Oscar's orange boats, decorated with raffia daisies. Oscar dribbles a little at the sight of her shapely body and pats himself on his back for being in the right place at the right time. That was last Tuesday, after Quiz Night, at The Rising Sun.

Yellow

Ruby yells. No-one hears. She is choking no more but is turning a jaundiced shade of lemon as she gasps for help. Yanni just happens to be in the street below blowing up golden yellow balloons to sell to the unsuspecting parents of children in the water park. He hopes the children will not hold on too tight to the strings for fear that they may get carried up and away—what he really hopes is that they will let go and scream blue murder for another.

He does hear Ruby's urgent pleas, ties his bunch of ready-inflated balloons to the wing mirror of his pale primrose Mini, and breaks into the flat. He proceeds to give her mouth-to-mouth until he gets a sliver of cream cracker between his teeth.

Yanni is not simple, he is a graduate of neuroscience for which there seems to be no lucrative opportunities hence his ballooning balloon business.

He rolls Ruby into a sitting position, attempts to put her head between her knees to no avail and so pops into the kitchen (which is piled high in dirty baked beans saucepans) to make Ruby a cup of Rooibos of which there appears to be none in any of the assorted caddies. "Let's go for ice cream," he announces. At which Ruby bounces up, pulls up her cotton socks and pops on her size 12 Clarks flatties with more enthusiasm than she's had in a decade.

Green

The green green grass of home slides over the horizon as the Green Lady II, a homemade sailing dinghy with Oscar and Ophelia aboard, slips into the sludge-grey estuary of the Humber. As they chug (yes they have a motor) under the Humber Bridge, Oscar begins to spout, "This is a one-point-three-eight mile single span suspension bridge and when opened in 1981 it was the longest of its kind in the world until 1998. It is now the 11th."

Ophelia has switched Oscar off. She sips her much-needed warming concoction that he's made with great aplomb (and the Grand Marnier) and adjusts her earbuds to get the full calypso beat of Yellow Bird with the velvet tones of Harry Belafonte. She's lined up a good playlist, still on her yellow theme for the mo', with Goodbye Yellow Brick Road and Yellow Submarine—she has deleted The Contradictions and Complexities of Yellow as it was far too confusing and did not blend at all well with the third Grand Marnier/orange/cinnamon cocktail. She switches to Mountain Greenery—always having liked Mel Tormé—and The Green Leaves of Summer by a brother-or-something band.

"Pheelie, that's Barrow Haven," points out Oscar. "Where the watercress meadows are." But Ophelia is humming along to The Shadows' Rhythm and Greens, with not the slightest interest in hearing about Oscar's gambolling through meadows, watercress or any kind, in his other life.

Blue

Yanni's deep blue eyes flicker and finally pull down their sleepy eyelids like roller blinds. He slouches with Ruby in blue striped deckchairs on the sea front in Skegness having arrived in the primrose mini, his bunches of yellow balloons diminishing with pops as the miles sped by. Ruby sucks on a blueberry ice lolly which is more a lilac colour than blue, 'but who cares?' Is Ruby's summing up.

She has already had a bag of chips with lots of salt and vinegar and Yanni is beginning to feel a fondness for this well-cushioned but potentially jolly, pink-cheeked companion with her bobbing golden curls. "Look," he says, opening his eyes to the ceruleanest of all skies above. A great blue heron soars awkwardly around them before cruising nonchalantly inland where it surely knows there is good feeding ground. "And look," he says again, as a light aircraft floats above, with the odd thrum, before their shielded eyes, advertising thirty-minute flights over the bay.

"Come on," says Yanni, "we are going up into the wide blue yonder."

Ruby is not about to argue.

Indigo

The sky has turned from clear azure to a brooding, bruised, grapeish shade as the Green Lady II heads out into The North Sea which happens to have turned into an ugly broiling turmoil with frothing jaws and black holes.

"We called it indigo," says Ophelia, "learned all about it at Art School."

"Didn't know you were an artist, Pheel," says Oscar.

"I'm not," she says, "just went for the good time. The wild parties. The music in the common room was always the best." And with that she replaces her earbuds as Mood Indigo is just starting. Tony Bennett was her heartthrob for about two weeks in her gay abandoned youth. A youth she is not about to share with Oscar who himself is thinking about turning back and ditching the woman who is turning out to be no help and not even good company. She hasn't even made him a bacon sarnie yet nor a mug of builders' tea.

*

Ruby and Yanni are high above the town, way above the bay and breathtakingly above the rest of the world as far as they are concerned. The pilot has warned them that a storm is forecast but he'll take them until they really do have to come down. It is a sweet little plane, Ruby has observed, even has a name: Sweet Violet. The pilot has handed them little cones with parma violets to suck in case they feel queasy and Yanni says, "Thank you kind sir, that's very thoughtful."

Ruby says, "When we have babies Yan, I think we'll call the first one Violet." Yanni squeezes her hand before spotting a small sailing dinghy beneath them in trouble.

"Mayday, mayday," calls the pilot, whose name is possibly Vernon, into his radio. "Boat in trouble—longitude erm, er, two two, latitude five three, I think. But I'm no expert."

Ruby and Yanni land (well Vernon does the actual landing of the Sweet Violet). They head back, elated, to their vacated deckchairs on the waterfront. They don't see the lifeboats setting out with their brawny crew and horns blaring.

All they see is the rainbow on the horizon.

33. The Miracle of Absence

It was the silence that filled her senses. No air moved. With the stillness, she felt as though she was frozen in time. Even the sea seemed stopped. There was not a riffle of a ripple on the ocean. She held her breath. She didn't even blink. She didn't swallow.

Then the red scimitar of the partially eclipsed sun rose above the ocean's horizon. The sky flamed vermilion and tangerine, reflecting in the sea. The sight filled her with dread. Filled her with horror. Filled her with joy. Filled her with overwhelming wonderment. She knew it was something she would never experience again. And she stood rooted. By the lighthouse. All alone. Not a creature moved. Not a bird sang. Not a leaf rustled. Not a cloud drifted across the pinkening dawn sky.

Later she tried to pinpoint the moment the birds began to sing again. But she couldn't. She wondered if—in that feeling of trance—as the eclipsed sun rose—she had been asleep. Even blacked out.

And then, like someone flicking a switch, all was normal. She heard the waves crashing on the rocks, and the chickadees chattering as always. She heard the traffic rattling on the highway, and the hum of the wires on the pylons. She put two fingers to the side of her neck, as she would at the gym, checking her heart rate—yes, she was still alive.

Amelia likened the experience to the world stopping. This is how she described it at the party the next weekend. They all laughed and told her to have another drink. Someone gave her a Blue Dragon in a conical cocktail glass. She swirled it first, listening for the swoosh of the shaved ice, before putting the rim of the glass to her lips, letting the hint of the Hypnotic touch her tongue. Letting the buzz of the jolly partygoers dissipate into the sensation of the drink's concoction.

Making the party-thrum fade. Allowing her memory of the dawn's eclipse to stay with her. Not wanting to let it go. Wishing the world could really stand still.

Even once a week would work. She thinks.

34. Three Anthems for Althea

There's no party for Althea's seventeenth birthday. No mother-baked cake. No giggling friends tittering over glasses of fizz. No puffed-up father jingling car keys from his finger, a pink envelope containing a driving school gift certificate in his other hand.

Nothing.

She doesn't cry. Doesn't swallow hard. She pulls her black toque down over her shaved head and buries herself in the cardboard box; all she wants is to be warm.

Anthem 1. Warmth:

A sun-filled kitchen with familiar pine table. Chairs with fat buttoned cushions picturing scarlet-sailed boats. Yellow striped curtains frame the window with views over the pasture. A chestnut gelding grazes, whinnies, raises his head, tosses his mane, in recognition of your birthday. The kitchen smells of coffee. And bacon. A brown dog stretches, raises his haunches, and comes to you, nuzzles his nose into your clasped hands.

"Walk, Bobbie?" you ask, petting him, your gold bangles chiming like a thousand distant bells.

His fronded tail wafts 'yes' and together you walk to the shore, over the dunes to the white sand beach. The ocean is flat-ass calm. The sand is hot. You dip your toes in the clear salt water.

Kicking. Someone is banging the cardboard box. Drunks drifting to another drinking hole.

"Gettup bitch," one says, baring his yellow teeth.

"Git outta there whore," says a second, gobbing green phlegm at Althea's shelter.

"Fuck off," she says, "get your own pitch, this's mine." She lets the glint of her blade flash. So they can see how wicked her steel is. She holds their stare. No one gets the better of Althea, a.k.a. Blades.

"Bitch," says the first.

"Fucker," she says.

They stagger off towards the canal, gagging on their dry smokers' laughter. Javex sucking down a drain.

Blades crouches. Her bony ass barely touches the wet pavement, but she feels damp draw up into her. She sets her knife on the sidewalk. Spins. Watches the flash of steel as the streetlight picks up its gleam second by second. Like an unwinding clock. It slows. Then stops. The tip pointing at the tavern.

Anthem 2. Wanted:

He's tall and fair with blue eyes. His smile is wide. And white. He's in a tux, waiting for you at the bar. His name is Christopher.

You're in the emerald silk birthday dress your father bought. A wrap-over, revealing a hint of pale young breasts in cream lace. Matching panties you don't anticipate being seen, let alone hastily ripped off, this night. That's the future. You wear your namesake grandmother's ammonite necklace. And the diamond earrings from your mother. You hesitate before joining your date at the bar; you need to savour your perfect birthday day. From breakfast in the sunshine kitchen. To Mother's excitement over the birthday cake, "Sweet Seventeen" in flowing pink script across the top of the cake. Edged with pink sugar roses. And Father, ruddy-faced, thrilled with the silver Echo convertible parked outside. For you. But best of all, your walk on the beach with Bobbie.

And now it is the evening, and here is your beau. Wanting you.

Blades hangs around behind the tavern, waiting for someone coming out for a smoke. Hoping she can bum one. The yard stinks of piss among the kegs and barrels. The door grinds open. It is beginning to rot at the bottom. A guy comes out, he is bald with grey chin stubble. He wears a scuffed black pleather jacket and drooping jeans, his crotch exposed. He scratches his matted belly and unzips his pants. Blades stays in the shadows. The guy pisses inches from her feet, the steaming spray catching her cargos and boots.

"Hoy," she hisses, "don't you piss on me."

The man passes a nitrogenous fart. Goes back into the tavern. Blades still hangs back in the shadows. Three men now, the third kicking the door. It splinters more.

"Here's the bitch, just like Biff said."

"She's all bones, it'll be like fucking nutcrackers, but hold her down, she'll do."

The third unzips his pants.

Anthem 3. Loved:

Christopher carries you in his arms. His minty breath whispers across your cheek. You've danced the evening away between wine and lobster. And the shared tiramisu. With two spoons.

He sets you down on the beach. Reads a poem. "I've written this just for you," he says.

His soft voice tells you you're his reason for being. Comparing you to early morning birdsong, to sunsets, and all things between.

He kisses you with cautious dry lips, winding a stray tendril of your shining brown hair around your ear. You hold hands, lie back on the warm sand, watch the moon over the ocean, hear a distant loon's cry. You know you are loved. Not just by Christopher, who makes promises, but by your family who will wait up for you until your beau brings you home.

There, after hugging, you'll cluster around the kitchen table with cups of tea poured from a willow-patterned teapot. Grandmother and Mother on one side; anxious to hear. Father opposite; furrowed brow. You'll tell them almost everything about your evening.

Blades drags her cart through wet empty backstreets. The wheels rattle over the ruts, racketing like a dozen skateboarders. She pulls her black toque down over her shaved head and moves on, one day older, into the murky dawn.

35. Pictures (and a few other objets d'art) for an exhibition.

(A novelette in 15 flashes)

One. Jesus

In the beginning, man was created in an image. By 'man' of course there is a need to respecify, to be pc. But this is very much a person of male gender on the illustrated cover of your book-of-prayer with its leafy-kelly's-green mock-leather spine and glossy frontispiece. A little book that fitted snugly in your best navy blue (itchy) wool suit pocket every Sunday morning. The book you were given when you turned thirteen. He (the bearded man in the night-gown on the cover) is finely water-coloured with pink cheeks and grey flowing beard and is fluttered around by chubby winged cherubs. While fluffy, happy, Bob Ross clouds smile down.

It is (not quite) the only thing you remember of that 13th birthday gift. You've forgotten all but a very few of the texts therein: The Creed, maybe; The Lord's Prayer, difficult to forget the rhythm, much as you try. No, it is the Image that embeds deep in the memory.

And that, as they say, is the power of a picture.

But also (here you swallow hard), the power of memory of disappointment when you didn't get the purple Raleigh bike you really wanted.

Two. Still Life with Plaster Cupid

Oh dear, Paul, did you pick that plaster cupid up at a yard sale? He's an ugly bugger isn't he? Spoilt kid's got nothing on him. Having said that, being armless probably gives him the right to pout, to puff out his little pasty cheeks and let them droop into his neck and chest like a baby Winston.

The minuscule penis might have something to do with his expression of acceptance too. An almost, 'it is what it is', look.

But there he is still, placed among the peaches and pomegranates as if waiting for you to feed him, morsel by juicy, dripping, honey-nectared morsel. You probably needed to mop up his little chinnie-chin-chin over the years too.

Do the shifting perspectives indicate he moved during the process of the painting? Shuffled around a bit like most models? The fruit probably ripened and was eaten, but should cupid be on the turn too? Was he looking at you, for you. Or was he actually looking after you?

He's been a trusty model for you I know, popping up all over the place in still lifes, adorned by rosy apples and glistening oranges, velvety draperies in muted shades, a perfect and complex contrast. The fruit full of life and taste for the onlooker to swallow and imagine, against the dryness of his plaster, of the stillness and longevity—as he will never age as we know it—but stay this solemn cherub with a knowing countenance—over the decades and centuries he will witness it all.

Be aware, Paul, you are being watched.

Three. The Burlington House Cartoon

Mister genius artist, you've done some erasing there, haven't you? What with? Did you have India rubbers in your day? Did you use fresh bread to rub away the charcoal? Didn't work too well, did it? What was there is still there. You know that, right? But it is pure genius to let us know your thinking.

Silence. Stillness. I breathe out. And in.

And what the hell is with the big, detached hand then? Slapped it in as an afterthought?

He speaks then. Gently, but still I jump. "It's the message," he says, "the essence of the drawing is in the hand. Don't you get it? Saint Anne is supposed to be pointing to heaven, telling his mother, 'It's his destiny'. Look again."

Following the oversized unblemished finger I can only see a mess of frustrations. Of scratchings out. Reworkings. Doubts. Corrections. Questions. No answers. Could the genius have had an unclear mind?

The index finger still points. Up. Insisting. Almost rude. It's as well it's not the middle finger or you really would have a message for us.

He laughs, coughs a rough cough, "There's a spare foot too," he says, "Did you miss that?"

Clever that, taking attention away from the floating hand. Down through the Mona Lisa smiles, (one knowing, one receptive) of the women and the typical wriggling cherubs (one looking upon the other with early signs of envy?)

But feet? There is just one; slender, barely attached to the ankle. Very clever Mister genius. What did you know? Why have you brought to me this family? Of mother daughter son. And cousin John?

"Look closer," he whispers, "at the spaces in between."

There are no spaces. Yes, under-stories in the scratchings and erasures. But skin touches skin. Thighs brush thighs. Limbs tangle. Arms hold all close. Breaths exchange. Eyes look into eyes. Is that a tear? This is an embracing understanding in all the knitted protective complexities of family love.

Mister artist, you are a genius.

Four. Rues des Moulins 1864 - medical inspection

"If you read the reports," he says, licking his already glistening lips, "you would think I have no feelings. They let me watch. As an artist I need to look. So that I can see. I understand parts of a woman's body that others probably only explore with sticky fingers and swelling penises. This is a Maison de Tolérance. These are the prostitutes who live close to where I live."

He recognizes them, he's rubbed shoulders with them when he's limped for his morning shopping at the market, ordinary women often with rosy-cheeked babes in tow. Choosing apples, selecting budding scarlet gladioli. And he does know the second woman in the examination line, the red head; he is her client.

Henri moistens his lips again, letting his tongue run around more times than necessary. He breathes in the familiar heady odours of Moroccan cheroots and jasmine-laced perfumes. The women he draws with his chalks have their jupes pulled up above their waists, revealing and preparing their body areas to be examined. He wills the red head to turn. To see if she recognizes him. But she looks ahead with a frozen stare, at the woman before her, the older, fair-headed one. He knows she knows that within moments it will be her turn to be scrutinized by men in white coats with monocles, who will probe her inner being with horny fingers, he wonders if it arouses the doctors as they explore anonymous vaginas. He hopes she is given the all-clear. He also knows how hard these women have fought for this service. To keep them safe and healthy.

It is her turn. He doesn't draw her while she is being examined, she closes her eyes. Henri closes his too. He hopes she is thinking of Toulouse.

Five. The Scream

Edvard, is this you? Are you so beleaguered by demons? What can we do to help? Is your world on fire?

I have chocolate if it will help, but then the image will bring your wide-open mouth together in a dog's arse pursing with screwed lips and still no teeth to see. Have you got any?

Were they all pulled out ready for dentures? Is that why you scream?

I have no answers for you Edvard other than to suggest you look towards your fjords and your snow laden mountains and feel their cool fresh air instead of this raging brimstone torrent beneath and behind you.

In the meantime let me find you a jolly frame to hold you close. And I'll come back, because maybe chocolate is really the answer. Or even a Cadbury's Creme Egg? It will fit your ovoid open mouth perfectly?

Five (a). Grinling Gibbons' Frame

We are going big and gold and curvy and shiny with this one. It should pull out all the fire tones of The Scream. And spread them to warm the world. Curlicues of ribbons entwined with rosebuds and bulbous grapes too large but perfect. The gilded carved wood with, are they angel wings at the top corners? seem to lift Edvard and help him out of his doldrums.

Maybe Grinling did you a favour, Edvard, when he carved this almost 200 years before you began to scream for it.

He heard you, take it from me. The frame has saved you.

Six. The Fighting Temeraire

Take a deep breath. This was the painting that caused our mothers to get themselves all aroused as teenagers. You must remember these were girls who would embrace soldiers, sailors, and fighter pilots before they were out of their teens. The uniformed and moustachioed young men from over the sea. Arousal was bubbling away beneath their surfaces of these girls.

There is sound to add to the senses in this gallery. Verdi's Grand March from Aida, written over 30 years after our dear JMW painted the grand old lady, HMS Temeraire, 30 years after as herself was tugged to be broken up. No matter—here she is preserved for you.

Turn up the volume now, feel the resistance to the tug. Sense her objection to being ruptured, yanked and split.

But mostly, feel for your mothers and grandmothers. Feel their arousal at the wild colours, at the turmoil within. Feel their resolve to remember this grand old warship and all she had been through.

No veterans' home for her. No floating restaurant in Manhattan. She is gone.

But she is not. Take another look. Listen to Verdi. And take heart.

Seven. Man Lying on a wall

When your work pops up on tea towels you wonder where it will all end. When your images appear in gallery gift shops on crockery and trinket keepsakes, you have to stop and ask yourself, 'Did you give permission for your man to wrap himself around coffee mugs, for people to dribble their spittle over your man's wall? Over his umbrella? And his briefcase? And, is he really *your* man at all?'

He looked at peace, your man on the wall, escaping the stench and raucous nerve-shattering noises of factories belching smoke. It seemed the world had gone to hell. But he'd found an escape. He was your man. It was your wall.

You saw the man from a bus window as you made your way home. Just lying there. On that mesmerizing brick wall, the one capped with white tiles. He was (seemingly) in an out-of-mind state. Your bus chugged you on home expelling fumes of diesel and he was left there. On the wall. Oblivious to the world.

And you envied him. When you painted him, as paint him you couldn't not, you felt as if he were you; putting down your brushes, your paints, and climbing onto your bed, lying down, taking the deepest breath you've ever taken and watching the ceiling become your new sky.

Your man is gone, but he is everywhere. On office walls. On shopping bags. On tee-shirts. And yes, on tea towels and coffee mugs. It seems that money talks now. You suppose you shouldn't have let your man go. For a pittance too.

Is there never to be peace?

*

I'd hoped for a blue endless sky. It'd been a pig of a day at the office. Numbers still danced in my mind like the whirling dervishes I'd seen in a news magazine; blurring, whipping, never still, leaving my head in a turmoil. The clean lines of the wall offered reprieve. A place to think.

Carefully propping my umbrella and attaché case against the wall I climbed aboard, lit a cigarette and lay back seeking answers in the grey smog of sky above.

Until a bus rumbled by snorting fumes. I saw him then, the funny little man who stared at me from the bus window, even as the bus rumbled on, he stared back as if he'd never seen a man lying on a wall.

Will I never find peace?

Eight. My Parents

"Here's a good one, Laura, listen to this," Kenneth jerks the pages like would a man sitting in a cramped railway carriage, and begins reading from the morning paper. "There's a new little car out, a Ford Fiesta, sounds zippy, should we go and look at one?"

Laura sits upright on a folding wooden chair, she's in a periwinkle blue dress which somehow gives her complexion a ruddy aura. She clenches her teeth and wonders why they can't have comfortable furniture before looking at a car. What would they want one for anyway, they don't go anywhere.

"We could go places," he says, as if reading her mind. He looks up.

"Dad, please don't move," says his son, the artist, who is splashing bright turquoise paint, or is it that Kelly's Green again? all over the kitchen floor. I just want to capture that stance, please keep looking down at the paper."

Laura hasn't moved a muscle, well, maybe a little twitch of annoyance at the paint on the floor, but her love for her boy far outweighs any paint. "Can I just move a hair...?"

"Of course, Mam," says the golden-haired son. "Why don't we stop for a cuppa anyway in a mo, I know I could do with one."

A red petal has dropped from one of the tulips in the powder blue vase on the (newly glossed from dark oak to turquoise/Kelly's Green especially for the portrait painting) table. "Shall I move it?" says Kenneth, "Will it spoil the painting?" He looks up, his wife is no longer sitting upright on her wooden folding chair, his son is no longer at his easel splashing paint around. He hears the kettle begin to whistle in the kitchen. He hears them laugh together.

"Look at this," he says, in a gustoesque fashion, brandishing the paper.

Laura sees a photograph of the Canadian Prime Minister doing a pirouette behind Queen Elizabeth.

Kenneth points at the headline: Manchester United win the FA Cup.

But the son, flicking his blond mop out of his face, is drawn to a quote from Gay News with a statement from Mary Whitehouse.

Nine. (Has been removed and taken to Wales (A WWII practice). Apologies for the disappointment. When this war is over the Paul Nash will be returned.)

Ten. Brillo Boxes

You were seen, you know, Andy, trundling your cart around the aisles of the supermarket, with Brillo boxes heaped high. Not stacked neatly as one would expect of you; Mr. Precision personified. No, these were all higgledy-piggledy. Precariously balanced.

And now this. Four high. Two across. Red, white, and blue. '24'. 'New!' 'Giant size pkgs'. 'Soap pads with rust register. Shines aluminum fast'.

Perspective precision perfected. Were you happy with the results? So, why did you need to do them over and over? In silk covered plywood? With house paint?

But why do this at all? Why replicate Brillo boxes? The aesthetic value is lost on me. Is this art imitating life? Like Campbell's soup cans? Like Heinz ketchup bottles? Is there a beauty I am not seeing?

And is there a copyright issue?

Marilyn would know.

Eleven. David

What a gorgeous young man you are. Unblemished in life. Unblemished by death. Here for eternity. Three times your own size, all ready now to lay any Goliath that stumbles across your piazza, yes? You look over the crowd's heads at something beyond our imagination. Something distant, ethereal, something from the past you wish you could change? And you're not telling. Are you?

You can you know, make those changes, with those veins that still pulse across the back of your hand. Still throb through your neck. Determination is there too and evidence of deep thought. Come back to us David. We will listen.

Twelve. Little Owl

Oh Little Owl, how Albrecht has captured your intensity. Your stillness. Your fixed gaze. As if you are porcelain. But breathing; living. How time stands still with your stillness. 1506 or 2016 it makes little difference. Your beauty, your steadfast demeanour, your stance aloft above us all. Your knowing and wisdom. Isn't that what they say? The wise old owl? But yours is more than wisdom. Yours is judgement and decisiveness and aim and precision as you see the velvet of the vole beneath the curling crisp autumn layer of fallen oak leaves.

No, please don't take flight just yet, give me just one more moment to marvel at your presence. The presence that causes me to stop and honour those like you. To hold breath and be thankful for your aura.

You don't turn your head but you know the great blue heron, for instance, stands behind and below you in the shallows, watching, waiting for the movement of small fish, those silver slivers, who in turn see, but don't see, as they flicker between the greenness of water weeds and rocks—shoals, hunting their own sustenance.

But you, oh Little Owl, you see it all. And you see me, I know. You saw Albrecht with his pastels and his paint brush, but that evening you did as was asked. You stayed and posed as the master applied each perfect feather, as he added the dry glint in your eagle eye, the claw-like hook to your beak echoing the beak-like claws to your feet as they confidently hold you on the branch of that autumn tree.

Capturing you for us to marvel more than five hundred years on, but still you have your freedom.

Twelve (a). Young Hare

A little owl and a young hare can only have one outcome.

Thirteen. Whistler's Mother

"Will you turn and look at me, your son? You are fixed, fixated. Feet together, clenched buttocks no doubt too. Auntie Dora's lacy curtain draining any colour from your cheeks. Mother look this way why don't you?"

You turn then, soften, let your hair down—flowing down your back in waves like the soft clouds above us that day of our picnic When we sat on the lush grass with the blue jug of lemonade and tomato sandwiches. It was the day we buried him.

He came to me in the darkness, I didn't understand what to do. We were married in the chapel just that day with bells ringing and people wearing smiles. And hats with lilac lace. I thought how happy we were and would be.

He came to me in the darkness, I had no idea what was to come. We'd feasted on tiny cakes and apricots and danced to the fiddlers tunes until we just had to sit and drink the porter that had been poured for us.

He drank many of those.

*He came to me in the darkness and told me what I must do.
We'd had a happy evening following the ceremony and the party.
We'd touched finger tips, his rough, calloused from working the
fields. He'd rubbed his fingers up and down my thumb as if I was
supposed to understand a signal.*

*He came to me in the darkness and ripped from me my pretty
silk dress my mother and Auntie Dora had made, sitting up nights
sewing by candlelight until their eyes were too tired to see.*

*I couldn't see him in the darkness. But I could feel his heavy
fatness drilling into me. I could hear his animal snorting, like our
pigs in the barn at supper time. And I thought that I should stop
thinking. To close my eyes and imagine this field of daisies where
we are now, James, my dear boy, and to dream of happy Bob Ross
clouds and hope that this was not the norm for a young newly
wedded girl.*

*In the daylight there was blood. In the daylight I couldn't cry.
I couldn't speak to a soul. I wondered who had bled. In the
daylight.*

"I see why you have no joy, Mother. Why you blamed me
who came along just months after that night of darkness and
blood. I was the cause of your pain.

Let me re-tie your hair, Mother. Look straight ahead,
while I finish your portrait. The gallery is waiting."

Fourteen. Persistence of Memory

There's a clock on the wall. It moves. Not just the hands. Not just the tick-ticking of the second hand. Not just the tip-tap of the pendulum. Not just the bing-bong of the chime. Look away. Look back. Isn't that the most amazing sensation?

It's moved again, folding in on itself as if of molten gold, its face contorted, arms pleading for help. Wrapped around death. Oh, midnight is it? Or is it time for lunch? No matter, we will just hang it out to dry over a birch tree branch and pop back and see Jesus in the annex. That is if he's waited, there was a feeling of time running out there.

Is time running out here too? Why are we all running? Are we not supposed to be following silken trails or sooty footprints?

Fifteen. The Head of Invention—James Watt

Yes, Eduardo you did boots, loads and loads of boots, I almost felt like singing a Nancy Sinatra song when I saw the array at The National. I have one. It is made of cardboard.

But this fella takes the biscuit. Or should I say biscuit barrel? He is all nuts and bolts and grommets and rivets. He is all parts and pieces. And yet he is whole. All three metres of him. That's some big head propped up on timber bigger than railway ties.

We saw what you did with David. How you took him apart, tied him back together with string. (Viewers, if you'd like, you may retrace your steps and view again Michelangelo's original David). But here with your bronze, sectioned with such intent, you have partitioned the head of James Watt (and it is disturbing), his is your Head of Invention, in between those subtle and quite natural (imho) sections you have slotted, in the incisions, parts of a quotation. Do I see something from our old friend Leonardo?

But let's look at the back. The inner workings of the head are exposed with cogs and wheels representing a very clever brain. Yours? Or his? Can we assume both?

Who knows what Mr. Watt would have made of this, but Mr. Paolozzi this is better than a boot. And it most certainly is not cardboard.

***

And so dear viewers we are at the end of our tour of Pictures and other objets d'art.

Apologies if it is raining —the Renoir room has closed for the evening.

Please send in your appraisals before the end of the year to be entered into a draw for a Lowry tea-towel.

36. Delphine's Bridge

The bluesman sings *Delphine* into the dark. Watching nothing. Rolling his tongue around the lyrics. His eyes close, in slo-mo, as the harmonica weeps its way in with the bridge—asking questions—where has she been and why don't she love him no more?

He sees her then, red-haloed-lit, under his eyelids, *Ain't had no lovin'*, he nasal-sings. *Why dontcha come back to me?*

Delphine listens inside the dark. She opens her mind at the bridge when she hears the weeping. It is time for her to sigh, to dream of gondolas, to draw back the yellow curtains while the world still sleeps.

The bluesman sings into the dawn. Watching the apricot of waking skies. Wanting to know if she hears his lilting asks. Not knowing he should look up. If he looked, he would see.

She stands midway on the bridge. Near yet far. Squinting down on the ripples arrow-heading beneath as the bluesman works his way through green waters, reaching out to grey ancient arches. Hoping to catch echoes of her replies.

Delphine needs the song to change as it travels beneath the bridge, for it to leave the minor whining key and lean towards the chorus to sing, *oooo-oooo, I will still love you…* For the dark conflict to go and for technicolour to lift her dreams away.

She is not caught in the culmination of filaments now, but in the space where neither can reach. In the gap of independent isolation. Not stretching out to the dark hues on her left, or to the rich vibrancy on her right.

Neither hearing, nor seeing, Delphine embraces her bridge, seeing her own path.

The bluesman sings on into the gloom as the harmonica weeps.

37. Round Robin, a novelette in flash (in two parts)

Preamble

People say Abbey-Saint-Vincent is stuck in a time-warp. But the villagers like it that way. They are proud of the butcherthebakerthecandlestickmaker continuance. They like buying a real newspaper to read on the wooden park benches (with brass memorial plaques) overlooking The Common. They are fine-tuned to their own church campanologists putting on a jovial peal of bells on a Sunday morning, accompanying big breakfasts and prepping of Sunday joints for the oven. They are chuffed to bits that Patsy's Tearoom still flourishes and Anthea-the-hairdresser's was taken over by Anthea's granddaughter Andrea.

Of course there's The Black Duck where male residents have their own pewter tankards hanging over the bar. This is where they talk in horror of the technology take-over and how they need to keep a tight hold of their traditional values. Many of the red leather bar stool occupants switch off and hide their mobile phones before entering The Duck.

The main players:

The Clarkes: Mavis and Peter and (probably even more pertinent) their son, Robin.

The Hendricksons: Angela and Tim and their son, Allan.

The Morgans: Jean and Graham and their dog, Pickles.

Part I

i. Waiting for visitors.

"What're we going to do today?" says the boy in the faded green tee-shirt.

There is no reply from his mother who stands at the kitchen sink peeling hard-boiled eggs, fart-like smells filling the air.

"Is that for my lunch?" says the boy, saying anything really, just to get his mother to turn and face him, to put down the eggs and their shells and for her to see that his lip is bleeding.

Without his telling her.

There is still no reply from the woman who has an itch she cannot scratch behind her ear because her hands are now (feeling quite lovely) in warm soapy water. She has finished peeling eggs and has buttered a mountain of thin-sliced wholewheat bread, two of the many things on her to-do list, before they get here.

"Should I change?" says the boy, conscious of his faded green tee-shirt and the mud on his knees from the fall that split his lip. The fall that came about because another boy wanted to fight him for his apple.

There is still no reply from the boy's mother. She dries her hands and unties her apron. Turning, she looks above the boy's head, through the window and out over the front lawn, watching for them to arrive, wanting everything to be perfect. For the table to be laid. For the hall floor to be dry from its morning mopping. For the sideboard to smell of lavender polish. And for Mozart to be playing at low volume as they walk through the front door.

"Robin," she says without looking at her boy, "don't forget to wash and change, they'll be here soon."

Robin slides from his kitchen chair and wipes the blood from his lips.

ii. The Visitors.

The Hendricksons pull up in their new electric Nissan Leaf in Cobalt Blue with BlueTooth Connectivity. At least that is what young Allan Hendrickson is all ready to spout to little Robin Clarke.

Angela Hendrickson straightens her shoulders. She has not been particularly looking forward to this visit, she wishes she'd declined the invitation really, with an existing commitment, or a pre-existing condition, either would have sufficed she'd told herself as she finished her hair with her new (secret) cordless tongs that morning.

A quick squiff with the latest organic fine mist hairspray and, "Let's go then, shall we? Get this over with." She orders Tim, her husband. "Find Allan, can you? I hope he's not dabbling in the pond again, he's wearing his new grey school trousers."

But now they are here, in their new car with its new car smell (with an after taste of hairspray). Allan's long grey trousers still have the front crease and Tim has applied his well-known countenance of geniality. Angela gathers them together like a shepherdess in a porcelain ornament and herds them, with difficulty and a few wobbles on her cream stiletto sling-backs (the front path is only 24" wide), to the shining royal blue front door.

Robin has been pushed down the hall (with its well-mopped, but now dry, floor) to answer the doorbell, he stands on tiptoes and unlatches the door, "Hello."

"What do you say next?" bellows a voice from the living room. Underneath the bellow, Mozart, is beginning to tinkle through the first bars of a piano concerto.

"Hello, welcome to our home," says Robin, aware now that the Hendricksons are large people and his neck is beginning to hurt from craning. "Please come in." He turns then and scurries back to the kitchen where his mother is piling egg sandwiches onto a red and white spotted platter.

"A minute later…" she says, "…and this lot would have gone for a Burton."

Robin has no idea what his mother is talking about. He has decided, in that instance, that this Mozart fellow is a pretty neat piano player, so wanders back to the living room where the Hendricksons sit in a row on the Wedgwood blue, corduroy three-seater sofa, a solid pine coffee table between them and Peter, Robin's father.

"Do you two know each other?" says Peter to Allan.

Allan fingers his bruised knuckles, Robin licks his split lip. Neither say a word.

"Then why don't you go out into the garden to play?" says Peter.

iii. Mavis gets her nails done.

The village now has a nail bar. It is in Anthea's the Hairdresser, in a small back room. Mavis has never had her nails done. Her appointment is for Thursday morning.

On Wednesday, Mavis peels enough potatoes to last the family for three days (so as not to get her nails scratched). She's dusted and polished, and persuaded Peter to take out the compost (which seems full of stinking egg sandwiches) and has decided that from now on, bed-making consists of pulling up of duvets.

On Thursday, as she walks in the pale morning sunshine, she's glad the village has kept its identity and not modernised, still has the traditional shops and churches. And the post office still has Heather, its jolly postmistress.

Mavis passes her old friend Jean who is going into 'Frankie, the Greengrocer's'. She knows Frankie cannot help the apostrophe—it goes with his occupation. Mavis also assumes Jean is going for a white cabbage—Jean is famous for her coleslaw. The last time she gave some to Mavis, Peter had the shits for days. But they never refuse a good-hearted, well-meaning gift, so they accept and add the coleslaw to their compost heap.

The compost heap is doing very well. Her boy, Robin, finds more worms daily, big fat ones, long skinny ones, and

Mavis watches him before school as he lets them crawl up his arms, shrinking then expanding like long thin pink concertinas, before placing them gently back on the compost heap. She has the feeling he talks to them.

Of course she always makes sure Robin scrubs with Dettol before he touches anything in the house. Especially their new upright piano. It arrived on Monday after Robin announced he would like to learn.

Anthea's is in the alleyway behind the newsagent's. Today's newspapers are outside on a rack and there, on the top, emblazoned in headlines is: *Young Boy Makes Fortune in Worm Business.*

Mavis can't wait now to get her nails done and get home with the paper. It is not her usual broadsheet. But this one she has to have, so she leaves the money in the honour tin beside the paper rack, and helps herself, folding it carefully so that the colourful front page won't be noticed, and so it will fit into her capacious beige handbag.

She chooses 'Pearly Queen Pink' for her final topcoat of nail varnish. The nail technician has babbled on about 'going out' and 'where are you going tonight?' which takes Mavis by surprise. She hasn't thought that you'd get you nails done to go somewhere.

So maybe she will. Maybe she can ask Peter to take her out for dinner. Then she can talk to him without interruption about worms. And about investing in a business for Robin when he is older.

And about piano lessons, because young boys need diversity in their lives.

iv. Missed calls and cabbages.

Jean Morgan pulls leaves from the outside of the red cabbage until she has a firm football of a vegetable of the deepest and luscious purple. Her mother gave her an automatic shredder for Christmas and Jean has used this to improve her cabbage shredding.

She cuts the big hard ball of purpleness into wedges and begins to feed the shredder. It is a noisy bugger and this is how she misses the phone call from her friend Mavis Clarke. Mavis wants to ask if Jean, and her better-half, Graham, would like to join her and Peter at the bistro on the corner of Market Street. To give it a try. The bistro opened a couple of years ago. Very much to the shock of the villagers when it replaced Bob's Café. This was after Bob dropped dead while installing a new-fangled cappuccino machine.

Mavis doesn't leave a message, can't leave a message as Jean and Graham don't have an answering machine.

The cabbage shreds soak in Jean's new recipe for brine. She has invested in new pickling jars and labels so that the pickled red cabbage can be bottled for gift giving. She has designed the labels herself using graphics skills she learned years before at art college in Bath.

While the cabbage soaks, Jean does the same. She has an affection for Badedas bath stuff. Apparently it has chestnuts in it. Jean read about it in Cosmo years ago, *Things Happen After a Badedas Bath*. Jean has tried it a number of times now, and so far nothing. Nothing. Jean lives in hope.

Little Robin Clarke has been knocking on the front door while Jean is in the bath. Graham finds the note on the doormat when he comes home from work. "We were invited out tonight," he announces, wafting the note under Jean's nose.

Jean's nose is full of chestnuts and vinegar and cabbage but she reads the note and wrinkles her nose, "Why?" She says.

Graham shrugs, "No idea," he says, "maybe they are celebrating something, but it doesn't say."

"Tighten these lids for me Gray, can you," says Jean. "I hope the little Clarke boy didn't come around to the side of the house, I was taking a very very long soak in the bath. I didn't close the blinds, the sunshine was so very lovely. Very. Lovely."

She leans against Graham hoping the Badedas will have the required effect.

v. Robin's win.

"I could see her titties," says Robin, eyes wide. "They are little, more like, well, splodges, not big and round like my mummy's." He rotates his hands.

"You're lying," says Allan. "How could you see? Was she sunbathing on her back lawn?"

"No, she was in the bath with no curtains at the window. They don't have frosted glass like us. I knocked on the front door with a note from my mother, but she didn't come."

Allan licks his lips, "Tell me more," he says. "Did she have those things on the tips? You know like round currant things?"

"They're called nupples," says Robin, "I think. Well, something like that."

"And?"

"They were very dark brown. I could see the detail. I couldn't take my eyes off. Then I heard Mr. Morgan's car come in the driveway, so I ran home through the back way."

"You were lucky," says Allan, "If he'd had an electric car like ours, you wouldn't have heard it. Next time can you take me with you?"

"Okay," says Robin. "If you stop picking on me."

vi. The WPS.

The villagers are up in arms. It is Saturday and a firm of developers is walking around The Common with mobile phones and digital tablets and big rolls of paper. 'Blueprints' someone said.

Graham Morgan, Tim Hendrickson, and Peter Clarke stand behind the cricket pavilion scratching heads and coming up with a plan of action.

"It will destroy the village," says Graham.

"It will ruin everything," says Tim.

Peter says nothing.

"Peter?" say Graham and Tim in unison.

"Sometimes the hardest thing to do is nothing," says Peter.

"That's what the Queen says," says Graham, "Jean told me. But how will doing nothing help?"

"Watch and learn," says Peter, "there actually is something."

They stroll over to their sons, Allan and Robin, who are playing conkers and annoying the Morgan dog, Pickles. Pickles jumps up and down and barks like a much bigger dog, like a Rottweiler or something, certainly not a little fawn whippet (which is what she is). They pat the dog, and then boys on the head. Peter says, "Give me your business cards."

The boys, eager to produce the new glossy chocolate brown cards with their names and initials WPS in embossed gold, hand them over. Graham and Tim look quizzically at Peter.

"Watch," he says, wandering over to the string of fresh-faced developers.

They look up as Peter approaches and try to shoo him off The Common. "Sorry fellows," says Peter. "Please leave The Common, this is protected ground right now according to the WPS."

The developers take the cards. Scratch their heads, go back to their vehicles with their blueprints, change out of their Wellington boots in their Landrovers and drive off.

"What..." say Graham and Tim, "...is WPS?"

"Didn't you know?" says Peter. "The boys have a little worm business. Their company is called The Worm Protection Society. Their headquarters is the compost heap in our back garden. But let these developers prove there are none of the WPS worms here on The Common."

The three stroll across The Common to The Black Duck where three pints of best bitter are already poured for them courtesy of the rest of the villagers.

The boys sit outside on the wall with a bottle of pop with a straw and a bag of crisps. "Cheers," says Allan to Robin.

"Cheers," says Robin, getting a nice warm feeling inside.

vii. Camping on The Common.

"Consensus: We have to protect The Common," reads Peter from the minutes of the village meeting.

It was a well represented meeting on Tuesday afternoon. The tea urn was kept busy, the home-made flapjacks, popular.

The chair, Tim Hendrickson, brought the meeting to order. The villagers—the men in sports jackets, Viyella shirts and old school or regimental ties, the ladies, in tweed suits, pretty blouses, and sensible shoes—listened without interrupting.

The agenda was simple: How to keep The Common from the bulldozer and a some kind of little-boxy housing estate.

A follow up meeting collected ideas on how to protect The Common. Some simple. Some complex. Jean Morgan was keen to plant cabbages. The idea was gently thanked and 'shelved for the time being'.

And so it came to be that the families rummaged through their attics and garages for camping equipment: heavy canvas tents, rubberised groundsheets, sleeping bags, camping stoves and clothes with lots of pockets.

They gathered around their campfire that damp night and before retiring to their tents for the night, sang 'Gooly-gooly-gooly-gooly watcha', with the ladies adding the 'ging-gang-goo' at the end of each line. The feeling was one of togetherness, of reminiscence, of childhoods long gone.

It was a combined feeling of taking ownership of the problem and finding a way through. The odd couple who surreptitiously swapped partners, slinking into opposite tents went, more or less, unnoticed. The village of Abbey-Saint-Vincent had bigger fish to fry.

viii. First night.

Mr. Robin Clarke, CEO of Superior Composting Inc. reaches across the massiveness of the king-sized bed for his new wife, Miranda. Her long fair hair, loosed from its anchorages of wedding paraphernalia, covers her face like his mother's old curtains in the spare room back in the stuck-in-a-time-warp village of Abbey-Saint-Vincent.

Miranda turns, smiles, "I really fancy a bacon sandwich," she says.

"Your wish is my command Mrs. Clarke," says Robin, picking up the phone for room service.

The tent flap flaps. Robin's bosom pal, Allan is spread-eagled on top of his sleeping bag. A cockerel announces a new dawn, a new day, somewhere quite close to Robin's ear. He watches the dribble running from Allan's mouth. He hears the gurgle.

Robin crawls from the tent onto the wet grass. He sees Mrs. Hendrickson's round behind bending over the campfire. A black kettle sings. But it is the sizzle of bacon that brings it all back, the wedding to a fair Miranda who has flat titties like Mrs. Morgan's, the wedding night in the big white bed with the view over a Mediterranean bay.

Allan joins him on the wet grass. Puts his arms around his best friend. Kisses him on the neck.

Robin feels a wobbly shiver in his belly.

ix. Nicer problems to have

"This is for grown-ups," says Peter Clarke to the boys. "Here, take these Tupperware containers and look for worms."

Allan and Robin know that Tupperware containers aren't the right tool for the job. Not when you've got explorer/fishermen style waistcoats with pockets and velcro fastenable flaps. "These are just the ticket," says Allan, patting his chest, when out of earshot of the grown-ups.

"What do they want to talk about that we can't hear?" says Robin.

"Aaah," say Allan, tapping the side of his nose, "something we, you and I, already know about. Yes?"

Robin taps his nose too, in a Monty Python sort of way. He has no idea what Allan is talking about. But smiles, happy to be part of a secret.

Heads together, the adults decide that if the leggy, new-comer brunette wants to crawl into old Aubrey's sleeping bag while Aubrey's Geraldine is asleep in her hair curlers, then that's their affair.

Ice cold Pinot Grigio is opened, paper cups held to the centre of their circle (avoiding the hot coals of last night's campfire) and a rousing, 'Cheers,' by all settles it.

x. All endings cannot be happy ones.

On looking back, Robin knows he was naive. He wants to be in love. But working with worms has a way of putting an invisible anti-social fence around him.

There have been birthday parties in the village to which he wasn't invited this year. But neither was Allan. His dearest and best friend, Allan.

They have built a den (camouflaged) in the copse on the edge of The Common. Here they meet. Talk. Sit. And lie down beside each other. Looking at acorns in the oak trees. Listening for squirrels. Laughing when the squirrels drop their acorns on them. Robin and Allan share comics, pop and crisps. And their inner thoughts on the world. Especially their world—the village of Abbey-Saint-Vincent.

Neither of them are bothered about silly birthday parties with jelly and balloons and Postman's Knock (although that did have a certain attraction). No, as long as they had each other. And their worms. Those were enough.

But the announcement that Allan was to go away to boarding school when he turned eleven—that kind of put the lid on things.

Round Robin

Part II

In which two boys overcome adversity using the latest technology. How developers and traditional villagers can put up a cracking good fight without fisticuffs, and how truth and honesty always wins the day. How one villager has breast implants (and counselling for her pickle-making addiction). And how the village of Abbey-Saint-Vincent finds they might have to move with the times.

i. Overcoming distances

"Hey,"

"Hey back atcha."

"Neat hey. This FaceTime thing?"

"What's it like there?"

"Miserable. Food's miserable. Dorm's miserable. Housemaster's a miserable git."

Robin wishes Allan would say, 'Miserable without you,' but Allan has looked away, there is a silence, then a wheeze, and Robin knows his friend's asthma could be bothering him. "Why don't you ask to come home?"

"Can't. I'll get ribbed for being a namby-pamby and have my head stuck down these grisly, miserable smelly toilets."

"Should I tell your mum?"

"Lord no. First off, they'll wonder how you know. Second, I have to see matron tonight to have my peak flow measured. She's not miserable. She breeds rabbits."

"Okay. If you're really sure. I'll send you something to cheer you up."

Robin packs up his experimental generation of worms in matchboxes with a little compost. He pokes air holes in the boxes. Then wraps them in large white handkerchiefs, then into a Scottish shortbread tin, and hopes Allan can open the parcel himself without supervision. He's pretty sure his friend will enjoy letting the pink worms explore his bed space in the dorm. And that Allan may even get admirers from the other boys.

But that last bit bothers Robin.

ii. No pistols at dawn

Village Meeting Regarding
The Common
7 pm Friday
Refreshments will be provided

The villagers gather early, chatting, hugging, excited to hear the next stage of planning the blockade. The blockade that will prevent developers from digging up The Common and building red brick houses with red front doors and postage stamp gardens with no fences on the seven acres that have been common land since The Domesday Book.

There is a rearrangement of the metal stackable chairs. The decibels, of the rattling of chairs, mask the sneaky shuffling-in of the developers who have brought their heavy gang.

But the residents of Abbey-Saint-Vincent have eyes in the backs of their heads and know full well that the aliens are at the back of the hall.

And their secret weapon, young Robin, is working his charm as usher. In a manner not unlike that of 'Bride or Groom' he directs people to their chair in such a way that villagers and developers are interspersed with each other. Eg. Villager.Developer. V.D.V.D.V.D.V.D.V… and so on across each row with each row alternating. No villager is next to a villager. And no developer is next to a developer.

Jean Morgan is in charge of refreshments. Her volunteers have made egg sandwiches, wafer thin slices of pork pies, mini Yorkshire puddings with horseradish filling, and, (well Jean couldn't help herself) pickled gherkins on toothpicks.

"Should I start the coffee machines?" Mavis calls to Jean.

"Indeed, yes please." Jean is in her element.

Angela Hendrickson is nowhere to be seen. She promised cupcakes with ASV (for Abbey-Saint-Vincent) curling in green icing on the top.

Mavis asks her boy Robin, "Can you see if Mrs. Hendrickson is on her way?"

Through the window Robin sees the Hendrickson's quiet Nissan Leaf glide into the car park and gives his mother the thumbs up. Returning to his alternating seating he is also thumbs-uppish about the manner in which villagers are chatting with developers in friendly ways and to such an extent that they begin calling each other by their first names and swapping gardening tips.

After the formal meeting is adjourned, smaller groups gather to chat amiably, gherkins on toothpicks are enthused over. Recipes exchanged. Unanimously, it is concluded that The Common will be safe.

iii. The truth, the whole truth and nothing but

Jean Morgan is a lady with a personal problem. Well, two problems really:
a) She wishes she had bigger boobs and
b) She can't stop pickling.

"Can you come round for coffee?" she says on the phone to her friends Mavis Clarke and Angela Hendrickson. After she's replaced the receiver, she wonders if she's done the right thing. She hasn't told Graham, her husband. She's whispered it into Pickles' lovely soft fawn velvet ear. Pickles is her whippet who has taken to peeing on the rug, but that hasn't fazed Jean one bit. She knows there are little pink pills that'll cure that. She just wishes sometimes they had pink pills for her. But, no, it's her other problems that keep her awake.

She pours coffee from her 1970s Portmeirion stoneware coffee jug. "Cream?" She asks, getting nods from Mavis and

Angela who both know that Portmeirion ware, especially like Jean's, with the botanic design, is fetching a fortune on *Flog It*, but say nothing.

They sip. They look at Jean. Jean fidgets in her celadon green tweedy armchair, "Erm," she says. "Do you two know anything about breast surgery?"

They look at each other. Aghast. *Cancer?* Is the question hovering on Mavis's lips?

But no—Jean continues, "I'd like to get bigger boobs," she announces, gulping down her scalding hot coffee and burning her tongue.

"Fabulous," says Angela, "my op was a great success."

Jean smiles, with a tremble of her lower lip, as Angela rummages in her handbag for her clinic's business card.

Mavis grins too as she passes Jean another card for addiction counselling, "For your pickling problem," she says, "I used these people when I couldn't stop crocheting. It really worked. Hope you don't mind."

Jean has faint recollections of Mavis's crocheting era. They all received red and green itchy cushions for gifts that year. The year after, it was yellow and blue.

Jean removes the coffee things and brings out a bottle of Cabernet Sauvignon 2017.

"We wish we'd told you sooner," say Mavis and Angela in unison, "all in this together. Yes?"

With a resounding "YES" they chink glasses and as their faces flush, they begin to share more secrets.

Unaware that young Robin Clarke is crouching under the window listening to every word.

iv. Around with Robin.

'Can I speak with Mr. Robin Clarke. Please?'

"I'm sorry, he's playing the piano at the moment and cannot be disturbed, can I ask who is calling?"

'Are you his secretary?'

Robin's mother, Mavis, leaves the phone off the hook on the hall table and wanders back to the kitchen where she is hard-boiling eggs for sandwiches.

Robin slips from the piano stool and with stealth (that he's picked up from his friend Allan), slides into the kitchen, "Is that for lunch?"

Mavis still hears the voice from the phone, asking if she was her young son's secretary. For goodness sake.

"Why do boiled eggs smell like farts?" says Robin, just to get his mother to turn and face him, to put down the eggs and their shells and for her to see his piano certificate. He hasn't told her about it. That he got a distinction in his exam. That he achieved the Mozart trills with great aplomb earning him extra marks. That he's been asked to play for a recital. He wants her to look at him. Now he is taller. Stronger. Now that he smiles.

To look at him without his asking her.

There is still no reply from the woman who has an itch on her nose she can't scratch because her hands are now plunged into hot water. She has finished peeling eggs, has made up her special curry mix for devilled eggs, and needs to scrub her fingertips that are stained like a chain smoker's.

"Peeeuuwwww," says Robin, "that's even worse. Should I wear a bowtie?" He wonders if he needs a black velvet jacket for the recital and if the mention of a bowtie will get his mother's attention.

There is still no reaction from her. She dries her hands and unties her apron. Turning, she looks above Robin's head, through the window and out over the front lawn, watching for her friends, for a meeting of minds, women's minds, wanting nothing to be perfect. To be free. She is planning for them to eat from trays on knees. To drink wine with abandon.

No Mozart will play. Boy George is all ready to play on the new Alexa.

Robin, meanwhile, is designing his new blog: *Around with Robin, a story of country folk.*

The village of Abbey-Saint-Vincent is beginning to move with the times.

38. Zinnia

The party is in full swing when Mrs. Zinnia Findlay steps out of the elevator. Her carer, Grace, gently supports her by the elbow. The community room is decked with Happy Birthday banners. Pink and purple balloons are tied around the room's ornate columns.

People cheer as Zinnia enters. They break into singing *Happy Birthday to You* accompanied by an old fellow on the piano. He has a silver moustache and a Harris tweed sport coat. He wears a yellow and blue spotted bowtie and a pastel blue shirt. As Zinnia looks across at him, he winks and twitches his moustache.

Everyone is seated in small groups at round tables with pink carnations in the centres along with battery powered candles. "Look Nana," says Chloe, "it almost looks real."

Zinnia nods. She's always thought things are either real or they are not. Like real butter and real wool. Just a small thing that made her grit her teeth in her younger days, only then she could respond. Now she smiles and nods.

It is a simple yet pretty party, with a selection of sandwiches: smoked salmon, cream cheese with cucumber, ham and tomato. There are tiny individual bite-sized pies too: cherry, apple, and strawberry. Pots of clotted cream with tiny silver spoons in them so guests could add a dob of cream if they wished.

"It's just as if I'd planned it myself," says Zinnia.

Grace nods in Chloe's direction, "Your granddaughter knows you well, she made all the arrangements. She loves you very much."

Zinnia knows, people don't have to keep reminding her. She knows they are being kind. She knows she seems forgetful. She knows names and words escape her. But she is still Zinnia deep inside.

Zinnia looks back at the piano, but the nice gentleman seems to have vanished. She could have sworn he was there when she arrived. But the music has stopped. Someone is banging a spoon on a glass. It is Grace. "It falls to me," she says, "to make a speech." Everyone claps. "Now as you know public speaking is not my strong point." Everyone claps again. "But I would just like to say that, since Mrs. Zinnia Findlay has come to live here with us, our lives have changed." The cheer goes up again.

"Zinnia has brought happiness to The Sunrise that we were all ready for. We were getting old and stale," she says. Grinning.

"Oh no we're not," is shouted from the back

"Oh yes we are," is shouted from the opposite side of the room.

"Enough of pantomime antics," says Grace, "dear Zinnia has brought us a cheerful capacity for fun and happiness that we will always be thankful for, and now it is our turn to give some back to her and wish her a very happy 82nd birthday."

The nice old gentleman is back at the piano playing *For She's a Jolly Good Fellow*, before standing up and bowing to Zinnia, "Could I please have this dance?" he says, with a wink as Grace loads the CD player.

Zinnia is sure she's seen this wink before. The yellow and blue spotted bowtie, too, triggers some deep memory. She would like very much to finger the silkiness of it.

"Hello sweet Zinnie," says the nice gentleman, "my name is Max and it is my pleasure to dance with you on your birthday."

She knows this strong hand that takes hers. There is familiarity about a callous on the thumb. She allows herself to be guided onto the floor, she rests her cheek against the Harris tweed and senses a fragrance long forgotten. And as Frank Sinatra sings, *The Way you Look Tonight,* she hears the soft humming from her gentle partner and feels a long lost longing.

39. The Carpet

Danush bows before his mother in a traditional farewell. The sun is about to rise. The sky is touched with hints of flame, indicating a brewing storm. Danush and his mother are aware that the weather makes no difference; they know he will not return until the evening stars shine upon the water.

"Spend your day well, dear son," says Fereshteh. "Drink much tea when you are allowed. And pray when you hear the call." She clasps his hands in hers, stroking her son's elegant fingers. "The work you must do is indeed an honour. But please save some strength for the future as neither you nor I know what it ahead for us."

Danush feels very grown up. At fourteen he as tall as his father who is in the hills with the goats. He has been charged to care for his mother and his younger siblings and is confident the dinars he brings home each week make the difference between starvation and survival. He may, today, even be able to get hold of some goat meat and milk for the celebration of his youngest brother's third birthday.

He is treated well by his masters as his nimble carpet weaving and knotting is far superior than any by the other boys working on royal commissions. He is permitted to stop frequently for glasses of warm sweet golden tea. Danush works alone on his carpet, which is unusual. It is entirely his work and when completed will be shipped to a king in a far-off land to grace his palace floor. There, the king's wives may recline and their many children may play with toys—something Danush has never had.

The boy cannot spare the time for fantasies such as these, much as he would like, as his long days wear on. It is enough for him to know his talents are recognized and rewarded. Rather than a large marbled palace floor, he would have preferred for the carpet to grace a wall, that visiting royal guests could stand back and wonder and, Danush's real hope, read and act upon the story Danush has secretly woven into the carpet.

Danush is quite sure his masters know-nothing of the additional minute images and hieroglyphics he has managed to integrate into the design. For Danush has another master; one who is instructing him to find a way to tell the world of their plights in this unofficial slavery.

He is sixteen when his carpet is finished. His back is bowed like that of an old man from crouching over his loom every day, the only relief is when he must prostrate in prayer. His eyes aren't as sharp as they once were, but his heart is light with the fulfilment and knowledge of his carpet being sent across the sea to the king.

***

Danush's carpet is loaded onto the steamship Clipper Montrose in 1859 heading for Siam, a place of which he knows nothing. His masters merely tell him his carpet is among the best they've produced and are going to the highest paying royalty. "We have received many dinars for them, we are happy. You boys may now go to your mothers and tell them you have worked well. We will certainly call upon you again." The boys bow.

Before returning to his mother, Danush goes to the harbour in Bushehr and watches the long teak boxes being hauled on board the clipper. He knows which box holds his carpet. It is clearly marked with 1. He interprets this as being 'the first—the best' and reports to his other master that the messages are now sent across the seas. "You have done well, Danush," they say, "you will receive your reward in heaven."

Danush returns to his mother while the sun is still high in the sky. As he climbs the outskirts of the village he looks down and sees the clipper steaming out to the open ocean. He lifts an acknowledging hand but feels part of his soul is embarking on an unknown journey.

Fereshteh is happy to see her son. She feeds him goat's yoghurt with pistachio nuts and dates. She bathes his gnarled finger joints and calloused fingertips in oil of roses. She brings his open hands to her face and kisses his palms. She soothes his eyes in a solution she has made with water from the village spring and sap from the gingko tree in the yard.

Danush breathes deeper than he has breathed in two years. His throat emits a rasping that fills his mother with a dread that her dear son has wool and silk fibres in his lungs. She knows this is the price for a king to have a carpet. She says nothing but smiles gently at her work-worn son and is thankful to have him home and not shipped with his carpet as she has heard could happen.

Fereshteh lifts Danush's head from the rough sackcloth pillow and draws the vessel of hot sweet tea to his dry lips.

He drinks.

THE SEQUENCE DANCE

40. Take a seat, Mother, see what I have done

You're taking her to the red sands shore. "No rush, Ma," you say, as she tries to finish dressing. Pulling on her best skirt. The one that reaches the floor. The cream flared one with swirls of red and green embroidery. The one you remember her wearing when you were in the school concert, when was it? Over thirty years ago now. She sat in the front row and clapped her hands raw when you played Joplin on the piano.

But this is the first time she has crossed the island since. You guide her from the parking lot, down the ramp to the shore where the plovers ripple back and forth. The gulls are busy ferreting through the seaweed. There is no sign of another living soul.

You assume the discarded chair has conveniently washed up with the tide. It sits in isolation between the dunes and the breakwater. It is one of those 1960s beach chairs with blue plastic strips that always stuck to your bare thighs. That was in the day, of course, when short shorts were de rigueur. The plastic strips are faded now, overstretched between the rusting metal frame. Hanging beneath. Pallid blue ribbons dribbling in the red sand. If a chair can take its last breath, this is it.

You lower Mother gently into the chair, wrap her long embroidered skirt around her boney white ankles, lest she catch a chill. Glad she has put on white cotton tube socks with her Duckies. "There," you say, waving out into the Northumberland Straits with a flamboyant hand. Wanting her to be amazed. "See what we have done."

She looks out into the clear waters, watches the gentle lapping of the waves. Her eyes flicker with the plovers. She studies the shoreline to her left, shielding her eyes, looking as far as Bells Point. Then she glances to her right.

"Oh, oh, oh." Her mouth opens. Closes. Her dry lips, her shrunken gums, her wide-open eyes that were once so green, now glazed. "Oh, oh, oh. Ach."

"Ma, what? What is it?" You begin to wonder if bringing her to Cape Travers was such a good idea. You'd wondered, briefly, if it would bring back bad memories. "Would you like to go home?"

"No, not now. What? Why? How?" She says.

And you realise she is looking beyond the breakwater to the bridge. The eight mile bridge you helped build. Your biggest career achievement. The bridge everyone takes for granted. Linking the island to the mainland.

You try to see it through her eyes, from the old chair sinking in the red sand: the sunset is obscured by concrete. The view of the distant mainland jagged, interrupted, incomplete.

The last time she was here there was no bridge.

You wanted her to clap her hands raw, but now you feel the desperate need to say sorry.

Acknowledgements

To the literary journals and magazines around the world that gave, and continue to give, my work homes over the years, that's the best validation a writer could ask. Thank you.

I write, for the most part, without conscious thought and thank two Canadian authors, playwrights and poets, Susan Musgrave and Natalie Meisner whose workshops all those years ago left their mark.

A giant thank you goes to my writer family: the members of the international online writing group, Pens Around the World.

Thank you to my loyal and oh-so-honest alpha and beta readers: Kat, Elke, Vicki, Marg, Pam (RR), Pam (S), Kimberly, J.P. Vincent, Bruce, Debbie, and John. Your eagle eyes are remarkable. And invaluable. Forever grateful.

To my flag-waver-in-chief, Vicki, for the hours, nay—days, weeks, and months when you've been there for me, extinguishing my doubts, cheering me on, and making me laugh. Non-stop showerings of love for you.

None of my books would exist without Arne. Thank you are words to small for your immense support, encouragement, astuteness and love. And for dragging me off down the coast for fish and chips when you knew I just needed a break.

To Summer Stewart for saying 'yes' to this diverse collection. And thanks always to all the team at Unsolicited Press for turning my manuscripts into books. For making them hand-holding real. And for making the entire book creation process an absolute joy.

And finally, thank you always to this peaceful corner of the world, where thinking, observing, dreaming and creating can happen.

About the Author

S.B. Borgersen is a British/Canadian author, of middle England and Hebridean ancestry, whose favoured genres are flash and micro fiction, and poetry.

Her books, *Fishermen's Fingers*, *While the Kettle Boils*, *Of Daisies and Dead Violins,* and *Eva Matson,* are published by Unsolicited Press. www.unsolicitedpress.com

Sue was educated at diverse institutions including boarding at a French convent in Nicosia, Cyprus before transferring in 1958 to a boarding school for military brats where she published her first story, *My Life Story: told by Laika, the Sputnik Dog* in *The Crusader,* the first magazine of King Richard School, Dhekelia, Cyprus.

Since 2000 her writing has won prizes, been mentioned in Hansard and published internationally in literary journals and anthologies. The list of publications is extensive and can be found at www.sueborgersen.com

She is a member of The Society of Authors, The Writers' Federation of Nova Scotia, Genre Writers of Atlantic Canada, and the international online writers' group, Pens Around the World.

Sue writes from her home on Nova Scotia's south shore with her patient husband and a clutch of lovable rowdy dogs.

S.B. Borgersen writes every day.

About Unsolicited Press

Unsolicited Press based out of Portland, Oregon and focuses on the works of the unsung and underrepresented. As a womxn-owned, all-volunteer small publisher that doesn't worry about profits as much as championing exceptional literature, we have the privilege of partnering with authors skirting the fringes of the lit world. We've worked with emerging and award-winning authors such as Shann Ray, Amy Shimshon-Santo, Brook Bhagat, Kris Amos, and John W. Bateman.

Learn more at unsolicitedpress.com. Find us on twitter and instagram.

Ingram Content Group UK Ltd.
Milton Keynes UK
UKHW040758250423
420747UK00004B/286